The Arranged Marriage

A BWWM Billionaire Romance By..

CJ HOWARD

Summary

Billionaire playboy Reed is loving life. Being the main heir of his father's fortune has meant he has enjoyed an easy time of fast cars, fancy parties and easy women.

*However, **all that is about to change.***

Reed's father is not happy about his playboy antics and he demands that he settle down or he will cut off his inheritance. In fact, he has already found the perfect woman for him to marry and it appears Reed has no choice in the matter.

Jillian is a beautiful woman of both African-American & Asian heritage. She is the daughter of very wealthy parents and so she is no stranger to the billionaire lifestyle. Reed's father believes this is the perfect woman to tame his son and make an honest man out of him.

Only problem is, Jillian and Reed seemingly can not stand each other. Can they put their differences aside for long enough to even make it down the aisle? And if they do, is it possible that true love can ever grow from such an arrangement?

Little do either of them know, there is much more to this "arranged marriage" then initially meets the eye....

Copyright Notice

Contents

Chapter 1

There was a soft knocking noise and a muffled voice pulling at him from the deep darkness. He tried to block it out but it became louder and more persistent. The sounds were like a dragnet that tugged and pulled at him, until finally the darkness surrendered to dim light and he opened his eyes.

The hair all over his face wasn't his. He blinked and wiped at the hair, trying to brush it from him but his arms felt like they were bolted down. He lifted his head slightly and looked around as best he could.

The hair on him was blonde and it belonged to the head of a woman who was passed out on his chest. His eyes moved slowly from her head down the length of her nude body and Reed smiled to himself. Beth, he thought, or Jamie. Something like that. The knocking sound and muffled voice persisted. He looked more closely at his surroundings. He was in a hotel room. His head was pounding fiercely and his ears had begun to ring. He realized that the voice was probably room service.

"WHAT?!" he yelled out and his head felt like it would explode. He tried to lift his right hand to hold it to his head but then he discovered that his right hand had been clenched around the neck of a glass bottle of whiskey all night and his fingers wouldn't quite move like he wanted them to.

"Sir, it's three in the afternoon, are you staying another night?" housekeeping yelled back through the door.

He closed his eyes to try to block the pain searing through his head. "Yeah! Yeah, I'm staying another night. Come back in an hour and restock the bar!" he hollered back.

He thought he would use his left hand to try to pry the fingers on his right hand off of the empty bottle of booze but then he realized that

5

his left hand was holding something soft and warm and he looked down to see that it was a large breast, and the breast was attached to a redhead lying on his thighs with her face on his naked groin.

He smiled again. LeAnn, he thought, or maybe Stacy. He was pretty sure her name was Stacy. He moved to lean up on his elbows, releasing Stacy's ample breast from his hand and using his left hand to pull the bottle from his right.

The girls stirred and woke up, looking around and then looking up at him. From the looks of it, and from what little he could remember, the three of them had had a very good time over the last few days. The blonde grinned at him and reached her face up to his to kiss him.

"Good morning, baby," she purred, smiling at him.
"I guess it's afternoon, honey," he said in a soft voice, kissing her back and fondling her hips and back side. He pushed himself up off of the massive bed they were all laying on and headed carefully to the bathroom. When he stood up, everything around him swirled and his mind went into vertigo. He stumbled backward toward the bed.

The redhead sat up and grabbed his waist, helping to steady him. "You okay, Reed?"

He rested his hand on her shoulder, hoping to anchor himself in the dizziness he felt. "I'm just leaning a little bit to the left, that's all." He sat on the edge of the bed for a moment and noticed a half full bottle of tequila on the nightstand. He grabbed it and took a long pull, then he set the bottle down and looked at the girls, who were both running their hands over his body in soothing motions.

"Why don't you two come help me to the shower, and then you can clean me off," he said tiredly.

They grinned and climbed off the bed, each one ducking under his arms and the three of them headed to the bathroom. Fifteen minutes later found the trio in the shower together, washing each other off and waking up a bit more.

Five minutes after that, Reed was thrusting a solid erection deeply into the redhead as she bent over in front of him, his hands clenched onto her large breasts, grunting in pleasure until just before he climaxed, when he turned away from her and the blonde swallowed his length, giving him such erotic bliss that he was only in her mouth for a few long moments before he released himself in her with a strong orgasm.

After their steamy shower, the trio headed back into their room and ordered lunch from room service. They were halfway through their meal and Bloody Marys when Reed heard a vibrating noise and found his cell phone underneath the pants he had discarded on the floor two days before.

 His phone indicated that he had missed several calls and texts and noted that his voicemail was full. He looked at the list of missed calls. Forty-two in the last two days, and all of them from his father. Most of the texts were from his father, but there were a few from one of his favorite girlfriends, Daisy. She wanted to visit with him. He smiled.

He knew he'd better get in touch with his father, so he told the girls to go ahead and finish lunch, and he strolled out onto the sunny balcony patio of the penthouse suite he was in. The bright sun was murder on his receding headache, so he sat in the shade of the bar and poured himself a Scotch before calling his father.

The phone didn't ring a second time. "Where the hell are you?" came the deep, angry voice.

Reed sighed and covered his eyes. "I'm just visiting some friends, Carter. What can I do for you?" He never called his father 'dad'. He had called him by his name, Carter, since he was a boy. He'd heard his mother call his father by his name, so that's what he called him.

"You can get your ass home immediately! We need to have a conversation. Why the hell haven't you answered any of my calls? Why are you avoiding me?" Carter asked, still seething.

Reed took a long swig of his Scotch. "I'm not avoiding you. My ringer was off. I'm sorry. Listen, I'll say goodbye to my friends and come home today, okay? Don't get bent."

Carter was furious. "Do not speak to me that way, Reed, you know far better than that."

He felt his stomach clench. "Yes, sir. I'm sorry. I'll be home soon."

"See that you are!" his father yelled and then hung up.

Reed set his cell on the bar and looked around at the stunning balcony where he was lounging. There were potted trees and hedges, flowers, bushes, his own swimming pool and bar. He glanced at the glass doors that led into his suite. There were two gorgeous models in that room waiting and happy to do anything and everything he wanted to do with them. He had a full bar and room service. He moaned dejectedly at the thought of having to go back to the house, but he knew he had to do it. He rarely disobeyed his father.

Reed sighed deeply and pushed himself up off of the barstool, stretching in the warm sun as his robe hung loosely on him, and then he sauntered back into the hotel room. The girls came right to him, wrapping their arms around him and kissing him on the neck and chest.

"What are we going to do today?" the blonde asked with a wide grin. "Can we go shopping?" she brightened.

The redhead reached her hand into Reed's robe and began to stroke his groin firmly.
"We could stay in and play some more, baby. Maybe get our party started early?"

She caught his attention and he turned to look at her wistfully. "I wish I could, honey." He lost himself for a moment in her big blue eyes and her hand which was wrapped around his stiffening bulge. He forgot momentarily what it was that he was doing. The redhead

8

let her robe fall open, taking Reed's hand and sliding it between her thighs.

"Come on, baby, let's play some more," she purred as she looked up at him and curved her full lips in a seductive smile.

He took a deep breath and tried to shake the hormones from his head. "I have to be going, actually. I'm…" He stopped as she ran her tongue up his chest and began to focus her hand much more intently over the rock solid hardness at his crotch.

"Come on, one for the road…" she whispered. "We'll make it fast." She grinned at him, pulling him toward the bed.

He could not resist her. She pulled her robe off and stood before him nude and gorgeous, her hands canvassing his body and pulling him tightly to her. The woman laid down on her back and spread her legs wide open for him, and the sight of it made him ravenously hungry for her. He was inside her in moments, pushing away, filling her with himself as she gasped and sighed in pleasure.

His hands and mouth covered her breasts, moving over them as if they were his only nourishment.

She clenched her body around his erection and he groaned as his orgasm drew near. He pulled himself from her body and she sat up and wrapped her lips around him as he pushed himself far into her mouth. She reached her hands behind his muscular hips and he cried out and orgasmed.

He looked down at her and she smiled as she wiped the back of her hand over her red lips. "See, baby?" she said softly. "That was worth staying a few extra minutes, wasn't it?"

Reed chuckled and touched her cheek. "Definitely. Thanks, honey," he said smoothly and then slid off the bed to get dressed. He combed his hair and splashed on some cologne, kissed the blonde long and hard, squeezed the redhead, and walked out of the door

9

saying, "You can stay one more night if you want to, but then you need to leave in the morning, girls. Thanks, it was fun."

The door closed and Reed walked down the hall with a headache and a full glass of Scotch. He walked to the door of the hotel and looked at the manager of the valet parking. "Would you bring my car around, please?" he asked as he pushed his sunglasses further up his nose.

The valet manager shrugged. "I'm sorry, sir, but you didn't leave a car with us. You parked it across the street from the hotel two days ago, but it was gone this morning when I arrived."

Reed was shocked. "It's a Ferrari! You didn't think that you should let me know my car was gone?" he raised his voice at the man.

The manager shook his head. "No, sir. I thought you drove it away."

Reed threw his glass of Scotch at the ground and it shattered, sending splinters of glass all over the drive in front of the hotel. The valet manager picked up the phone and called housekeeping to come right away, then he looked at Reed again. "Sir, may I be of any further assistance?"

Reed didn't answer him. He walked back into the hotel and went to the bar for another drink. He called the police and turned in a stolen car report, then sat in the recesses of a deep leather chair. He looked at his phone again, wondering if he should call his father to have a car sent for him, but then thought better of it and looked at Daisy's text messages. She had wanted to see him. He called her.

She answered after a couple of rings and she was excited to hear from him. "Hey baby!" she said as though she was glowing.

"Hi, bunny. How are you doing?" he asked, not really wanting to know.

"Oh, I'm good. I just got up; I had to fill in for one of the other dancers last night and it turned into a wild party after my show, so I slept late today. I don't have to go in until tonight. Do you have time for a visit today before I go back to the club?" She was a very talented and beautiful stripper, and the only thing he loved more than watching her dance was getting his hands on her afterward.

He grinned. "Well yeah, of course. I'm over at the Regent. Can you come pick me up?" he asked.

"Sure! I'm so excited to see you! I'll be right there," she gushed and hung up. He took a long pull off of his glass of Scotch and closed his eyes, resting them and trying to calm the storm in his head.

Half an hour and two scotches later, she waltzed into the bar of the hotel in a skimpy little silk shift with a hem that swayed around her upper thighs and clung delicately to her generously curved breasts that moved freely beneath the blue material. Her blonde curls were pulled up and pinned loosely around her head. As she came toward Reed, he saw that every man in sight was staring at her, looking, lusting, imagining, and he grinned at the thought that she was there solely for him.

When she reached him, she wrapped her arms around his neck and he slid his fingertips slowly up her thighs until they were just underneath the edge of the hem of her dress.

She looked up at him through her thick dark lashes and smiled warmly, her green eyes shining. "Hi, baby."

"There she is," Reed answered, leaning down to kiss her soft pink lips. His fingertips drew circles on her skin and moved to cup her ass and squeeze it gently. She moaned and slid her tongue over his sensually as she kissed him back. It shortened his breath. She kissed him again and then looked back up at him.

"I've missed you, Reed. It's so good to see you. Come on, let's get out of here." She winked at him and took his hand. He let her lead him out to the front of the hotel where her car was parked and he climbed into the passenger seat. She closed the driver side door and looked at him. "Where are we going?" she asked.

11

"I need to head to my place," he said with a note of disappointment.

She heard it and grinned at him, sliding her sunglasses on. "Well then, we'll just have to make a stop along the way," she said, with a sassy toss of her blonde curls. She drove away from the hotel and Reed looked out of the window for a little while, but Daisy was singing and dancing around her in seat, shaking her head of curls and her loose breasts under her dress, and Reed's attention was soon focused solely on her.

"How do you live like that?" he asked, enthralled with her wild, free spirit.

She flashed her wide smile at him. "Life is too short to care about the inconsequential negative crap." The wind coming into the jeep played havoc with her blonde curls, twisting them and tugging at them.

Reed reached his hand over to her thigh and slid his fingers up underneath her short dress until he felt the soft blonde hair between her legs. His eyebrows went up in surprise. "No panties, Daisy?" he asked.

She shook her blonde curls. "Not when I'm going to see you. Do you know how many pairs of really great panties I've lost because you've ripped them off of me in a moment of passion? Too many. I'm just practicing a little loss prevention here, that's all," she said, shaking her head.

His fingers caressed her softness and then found warmth and moisture and he began to massage her. She gasped and clenched the steering wheel. "Not while I'm driving! That's unsafe! You'll make me wreck!" She swatted at his arm.

He didn't listen. His fingers pressed more firmly against her, slipping into her slightly, and he leaned over and kissed her bare shoulder. She pulled his hand from between her thighs and pushed him away. "Wait till we get there!"

He cocked one eyebrow at her. "Get where?" He reached his hand over and began running the tip of his finger over her hard nipple as it pressed against the thin blue silk of her dress.

She let out a long breath, trying to focus on the road. "The beach."

He blinked at her. "I thought you were taking me home."

Daisy turned her head slightly and looked over the rim of her sunglasses at him. "I'm gonna have some fun with you before I let you go. I don't get to see you as often as I want to. I have to make the most of it when opportunity knocks and you actually call me back. Don't worry, baby, you'll love it." She blew him an air kiss and his hand cupped her breast firmly.

"Then get there fast already." He massaged her breast and she laughed at him.

"If I go any faster, I might get pulled over. Then I'll have to work my way out of a ticket with the cop. You don't want me to have to do that, do you?" she asked in a playfully warning voice, giving him a sidelong glance.

He shook his head and smiled. "No, I guess not."

Reed teased her body and aroused them both to the point that by the time she pulled in to a secluded area of dunes and trees on the quiet beach, they were both more than ready for each other.

She turned the jeep off and he laid his seat back a bit. She crawled over to him and opened his pants, pulling them down to his knees before straddling him lightly and leaning over to kiss him breathlessly.

Reed's hands moved up her bare thighs and closed over her hips, pulling her to his crotch, but she resisted slightly, running her tongue over his and kissing him deeply. She leaned up a little and looked at him, her green eyes bright with excitement.

13

"What do you want today, Reed?" she asked, her sweet sexy smile curving her lips.

He was so hungry for her at that point that he could barely speak to her. "I want to screw you until I can't move," he said in a hoarse whisper, looking up at her lovely face and squeezing his fingers into her flesh.

"You got it, baby," she said softly, lowering her body down over him and sliding his erection into her until there was nothing between them. He closed his eyes and began moving his hips, pumping them into her slowly at first, and then gaining momentum as his excitement caught fire, then he opened his eyes and pulled her face down to his to kiss her hard and fervently.

He reached one hand up to her shoulders and pulled at the thin straps of her dress until it fell from her and her perky rounded breasts were bouncing in his face. He groaned and closed his mouth around one of her nipples, sucking and biting at it, twirling the tip of his tongue over it, while his hands moved over her hips and her back. She just looked down at him the whole time, never taking her eyes from him as she rode him hard and fast.

Just as he was going to climax, he threw his head back and closed his eyes, gasping. "Now!" he called out and she lifted herself from his body and lowered her face into his crotch, sliding his erection past her lips and into her mouth.

 Reed cried out in immense pleasure and both his hands twisted into her thick blonde curls as his hands closed around the back of her head and he began pushing himself further and further into her mouth and down her throat. "Oh! Baby!" he cried out, thrusting his pelvis hard toward her face and pulling her to him urgently. "That's it! That's my girl…. That's… ahhhh!" he cried out as he ejaculated with terrific force into her hot mouth and down her throat.

His wave of pleasure subsided slowly and she withdrew him slowly from her soft pink lips and smiled up at him, kissing his thighs before she sat back up and pulled her dress back on.

He sighed deeply, satisfied and turned his head over to her. "What are you doing now?" he asked as she straightened her hair in the mirror.

"I'm going to take you home. Isn't that what you wanted?" she asked with a sly smile.

He stared at her for a long moment, wanting something else entirely. "No, I want to spend the day inside you, but I guess if I have to go, I have to go. Carter is insisting on it." He grumbled, leaning over and slipping the strap of her dress off of her shoulder. He kissed her tanned skin and then pulled her dress down until her breast came loose and he closed his mouth around her nipple, sucking gently at first and then harder as he pushed his hand back between her thighs and slid his fingertips into her, rubbing her body swiftly until she closed her eyes and pushed her head back against her seat, crying out as she arched her back and her orgasm swept over her, making her shudder, and making Reed hungry for her again.

She pushed his hand away and pulled her dress strap back up over her shoulder. "It's time to take you to him," she said quietly as she pulled her seatbelt on and backed the jeep out of its hidden spot in the beach dunes.

Reed frowned and turned his head to look out of the window. "I guess," he said quietly.

They were a short distance down the road when she looked at him and asked, "Why don't you ever come in me? Why do you always want to come in my mouth?"

He shook his head. "I don't want to have a kid. I'm just practicing a little loss prevention." He tossed her words back at her and laughed. She smiled at him and took his hand in hers, raising it to her lips and kissing it before letting it go and driving him home.

She turned off the main road and slowed her jeep down as it made the long rounding curve toward the enormous mansion at the end of the drive. She shook her head. "No matter how many times I've seen this place, it always intimidates the hell out of me. No one should live in a place that big. Seriously. It's just you, your dad and your brother. What do three guys need with that much room?"

Reed shrugged and sighed. "I have no idea. I'm never here." Then he looked around and saw that his car was parked near the garage where his father's cars were kept. "Wait!" he said sharply. "What's my car doing here? I thought it was stolen!"

Confusion rushed through his mind. He furrowed his brow and tried to remember if he had somehow brought it home, but he knew he couldn't have. He'd been at the hotel for three days and even the valet manager said that his car was there for both days until it had disappeared that morning, and he knew he hadn't driven it home.

He was at a loss.

Daisy leaned over and kissed him deeply, holding him close to her as long as she could, before he pulled away from her and waved her away, heading into the house, and in his mind, into the lion's den.

Carter was sitting as his massive mahogany desk in his large and stately office, working on his computer, when Reed walked in. Carter did not stop working to look up at him, but kept on typing while he greeted his son in a stern tone.

"It's about time you showed up. Sit down."

Reed sat down, his hangover still wreaking havoc with his body. He waited quietly for his father to finish what he was doing and turn toward him. It was a full five minute wait before Carter closed the screen of his laptop and turned to look at his son.

"You have truly hit the bottom of the barrel, young man. I've talked with you several times about your wild partying and carousing.

16

We've discussed the damage your actions and debauchery have done to tarnish the public image of our family and our business, and no amount of my intervention has made a difference to you.

"I can no longer give you a mere lecture or occasionally turn a blind eye. I can no longer leave it in your incapable hands to correct your errant behaviors. I can no longer continue to let our attorneys clean up your legal messes or produce the funds to repair the aftermath of destruction that you leave in your wake; particularly in the form of monetary settlements for both people and property. You are old enough to know and do much better than you've wasted your youth doing."

He stood up and walked around his desk, his eyes sharp and piercing as they held Reed's in a steady gaze.

"Have you seen the news today?" His father leaned against his desk and folded his hands in front of him.

Reed shook his head silently.

Without looking away from Reed, Carter reached back onto his desk and grabbed a stack of newspapers, which he tossed in Reed's lap.

"You've managed to expand your reach beyond the society pages and land on both the business and front pages," Carter said with quiet anger.

Reed looked down and picked up the stack of papers he was sitting beneath. There he was, staring at photos of himself. He was drunk in a fountain in one, dancing nude with the redhead and the blonde in a private club in another, hanging out of his car and vomiting in one, and making out heavily with both girls in a corner booth at a swanky restaurant.

They were clear pictures of what his last few days had been like, and he couldn't remember doing any of the things he was seeing in print.

He realized he should feel shame; that he should be remorseful, but he only felt like a hollow shell as he sat there silently beneath his father's reproachful eyes.

"Have you nothing to say to me?" Carter asked, his eyes penetrating his son as though he might find the answers he sought if he only looked hard enough.

"Nothing, sir," was Reed's reply.

"Well, Reed, I have something to say to you," Carter said, sliding his hands into his pockets. "There's a girl I want you to meet." His tone remained quite serious. Reed blinked in complete surprise. He'd been expecting another lecture, but nothing like what his father had just said, and certainly not what followed. "Actually, you've already met her, but you haven't seen her since you were children. Her name is Jillian. Her mother is one of my oldest business acquaintances and her family has considerable control over some of the largest technology companies in Japan."

Reed felt his memories sifting slowly through his mind, like sand in an hour glass, one by one, bit by bit, until finally the distant faded memory began to come back to him slowly.

There was a girl named Jillian. Her mother was Asian and her father was African-American. She was very different looking than other children he had known. He was a few years older than her, and when they met, he'd been fascinated with her. Reed remembered his father suggesting that he show her the gardens on the grounds behind the home, and he led her outside. She was quiet and shy, quite a bit smaller than him, and hesitant to follow him.

He had coaxed her outside and when they got to the garden, she was more interested in the flowers and trees than she was in him. It had frustrated him, so he had pretended to be interested in the jade bracelet she was playing with underneath her sleeve and he asked her to show it to him. She said she couldn't, that she wasn't supposed to have the bracelet and she had sneaked it that morning. He promised he would keep her secret and he begged her to take it off. She complied, removing it from her wrist and handing it to him so he could look at it. But instead, he turned and ran from her, laughing and looking back over his shoulder at her, wanting her to chase him.

She had chased him, panicked and crying, but she wasn't as fast as he was, and when he looked over his shoulder again to see if she was still behind him, he had tripped and fallen, and the delicate jade bracelet had flown out of his hand and hit one of the marble columns in the atrium near the garden.

It had shattered into several pieces and when he saw what had happened, he was afraid he would be in trouble, so he ran away and left Jillian there in the atrium among the shards of broken jade. He had never seen her again since, but when his father asked him if he knew anything about it, he had lied and said no. He'd been scolded for not showing Jillian the garden as he had been instructed to do, but that had been the extent of his trouble.

"I remember Jillian," Reed said quietly, watching his father in confusion.

Carter nodded. "Good. I want you to take her out on a date. It's obvious that you are spending time with the wrong sort of women and she is the kind you should be seeing."

Reed's jaw fell open. "Date her? Carter, I don't even know her!" He couldn't hide the shock in his voice.

Carter leaned forward and placed his hands on the armrests of the chair that Reed was sitting in. "I'd venture a safe bet that you don't know the women you were photographed with in these newspapers either, but that doesn't seem to stop you." His tone lowered slightly. "Let me make this crystal clear for you. You have humiliated our family. You have shamed our business. You have seriously sullied our public image. You have run out of options. Reed, you will date this girl, and only this girl, or you will find yourself without your car, like you did this morning, and without any finances whatsoever.

You will be forced to get a job, and as you have absolutely no work experience, you could reasonably expect to be hired at some sort of fast food facility or a big box discount warehouse store.

"You do not have a choice. You date the girl or you are on your own. Do you understand me, Reed?" Carter's face was inches from Reed's.

Reed looked at his father's eyes and realized that every word he had spoken was no mere threat. The concept of losing his precious red Ferrari was beyond anything he was willing to imagine, not to mention his enormous allowance.

Flashes of his wealthy playboy lifestyle vanished in his mind and were replaced with thoughts of him asking whether drive-thru customers wished for fries with their meals. He felt an untold horror rise up in him and he nodded his head adamantly.

"I'll do it, Carter," he said right away.

Carter stood up and straightened his jacket. "Good. I'll get you her contact information. Call her today and set up a visit with her immediately. You are finished with your wild ways."

Moments later, Carter placed a paper in Reed's hand and Reed nodded again and walked out of his father's massive office. His heart was pounding in his throat and blood was rushing in his ears. He felt like his whole world had just flipped upside down and ended.

Chapter 2

The two women stood together in the foyer of the tea house. The attendant came up to them and asked if they had a reservation. The older of the two women who was very obviously Japanese, nodded her head.

"We do, under Kimiko. My daughter and I are here for tea this afternoon," she said in a business-like tone.

The attendant glanced at the younger woman with widened eyes and then looked back at the older Japanese woman. She nodded, then lowered her head and led them to a secluded table. They were seated and a screen was drawn beside their table to afford them some privacy.

The attendant sneaked one more look at the younger woman and then hurried away. She was used to it, though she didn't like it. Jillian was quite exotic looking, and her looks had drawn the attention of people from the time she was a child. She had her father's dark coloration; her mahogany skin, full lips and black eyes were almost a replica of him, but her hair was like her mother's; long, black and sleek. It hung down to her waist like a thick flat curtain.

She also had her mother's high sculpted cheekbones and defined jaw line, as well as her very slight frame, so she was of a small stature, but she definitely had a black woman's curves. She had never seen another person who looked anything like her. She was alright with that, because she was constantly told how beautiful she was, but she felt like she was not really connected to anyone who was like her.

Jillian's life was steeped in Japanese culture and tradition. When her father had met her mother during the war and married her, bringing her home to the United States, he had adapted his entire life to suit her customs and culture. They lived in a house built in classic Japanese design both in structure and in landscaping. There were koi ponds and bamboo in the gardens, and her father had his own dojo which faced the gardens. She was fluent in Japanese and English, and though her world centered around that heritage, the only person she felt most connected to was her father. She felt like they understood each other more than anyone else in her family.

Her father knew what it was like to be black and she seemed to relate to him the most, though she deeply loved and respected her mother, she just didn't feel the connection to her Japanese heritage.

 Their tea was served and Kimiko sipped hers and then looked at Jillian. "I want to talk to you about something important." She spoke in a quiet and serious tone.

Jillian looked at her mother expectantly, as the tea cup sitting on the table before her sent steam wafting up near her face.

"I spoke with an old business colleague of mine recently. He has a son a few years older than you. You might remember him; we went to see him when you were a small girl and there was an incident with my jade bracelet. Do you remember that?"

 Jillian felt her heart clutch in her chest. She would never forget it. She had been taken on a business meeting to an enormous estate; a house bigger than any other she had ever seen. When they arrived, the man they had gone to see had suggested that his son show her the gardens. She hadn't wanted to go with him; she was shy and she would much rather have preferred to stay with her mother and sit quietly in the enormous room that looked like a library. But her mother gave her the look that she always gave her, the one that said she had no choice in the matter, and she grudgingly followed the boy out to the garden.

He seemed to want to play rough, to run and chase, but she was in a skirt and her best shoes, and she had no interest in it or in the boy. She loved seeing the garden and had felt like she had suddenly entered a safe and secret world where she could be herself and have no worry about others.

The boy had run off and things were quiet and peaceful for a few moments while she wandered happily through the beautiful garden, but then he came back and approached her slowly. He wanted to know about her bracelet. The delicate jade bracelet she shouldn't have been wearing.

She knew she shouldn't have it; she had sneaked into her mother's room while her mother was out, and had found it in her jewelry box. It was carved with tigers, elephants and dragons and was so beautiful that she couldn't resist lifting it from the box it was in and slipping it into her pocket.

She usually wore long sleeves on her dresses and so she was able to hide the bracelet from sight, but in the garden where she thought no one could see her, she had been holding it and tracing the carvings on it with her fingers, admiring it lovingly. The boy had asked to see it, and at first she had been terrified to be caught with it.

She slipped it back onto her wrist and slid her sleeve over it, her heart pounding against her ribs, but the boy softened his voice and became friendly, and said he only wanted to see it. She reluctantly pulled it off and handed it to him, so scared to share such an enormous secret, and the moment it was in his hands, the boy laughed loudly and turned from her, running away toward the atrium.

Fear exploded throughout her tiny body and adrenaline coursed through her as she tried to chase after him to retrieve her mother's bracelet, but she couldn't keep up with him; he was bigger and faster than she was, and when she caught sight of him again, he was looking over his shoulder at her and that was when it happened.

He tripped, and the bracelet went flying. It seemed to fly in slow motion, as though the whole world had stopped to watch its trajectory, and the whole world waited as it glided through the air; then there was a moment of deafening silence just before the bracelet hit the large marble column at the edge of the atrium.

Jillian watched in horror as the silence was broken by the clink of the bracelet as it collided with the marble and suddenly splintered into dozens of pieces, and all of them flew in every direction.

The boy lifted himself off the ground and saw the look on Jillian's face, and he bolted off away from her. She felt frozen as she watched all the pieces land; some bouncing off the ground, some breaking even more. She walked toward them and stared at them lying around her feet.

She knew deep in her that she had committed an atrocity against her mother that would never be forgiven, and it turned out that she was right. She tried to pick up all the pieces before anyone found her, but there were so many that just as she was getting to the last of them, her mother walked up behind her and held out her hand.

Jillian had looked up at her in complete fear and slowly emptied the contents of her little hands into her mother's. Her mother looked at the pieces and she saw an anger that she had never seen before come over her mother's face. Her mother had taken her home in total silence, and her punishment had been long lasting and harsh. She had never touched anything of her mother's again after that.

She looked at Kimiko. "I remember him." She said quietly.

"I though you might." Kimiko answered. "His father, Carter, and I were talking recently and we think that the two of you might make a good match. His father is a billionaire and owns one of the biggest technology firms in the United States. Someday, he will inherit all of that and operate it, as he is the older of his father's two sons.

"You are already aware that our family in Japan is one of the most influential and powerful technology manufacturers in the country. We think that aligning our households would be mutually beneficial to both families in many ways. I want you to meet with the boy and go out with him on a date." Kimiko stated this as though she had just told her daughter to go check the mail.

Jillian felt her heart begin to race and heat flooded her face. Her breath grew short and she looked at her mother with widening eyes. "Mother, I already have a boyfriend."

Her mother looked at her squarely. "Who is your boyfriend?" she asked, as though she didn't already know.

Jillian looked away from her for a moment and then looked back, wondering why Kimiko would pretend to not know. "Wilson, Mother, I've been dating him for six months now."

Kimiko closed her eyes and looked away, lifting her tea cup for another sip. "He's not your boyfriend. He's just a hungry little stray dog who is sniffing around you," she scoffed. "Please tell me you haven't actually taken him seriously."

Jillian drew her breath in slowly in a wasted attempt to slow her heart down. Everything in her felt as though it was racing and rushing underneath her calm exterior. She was practicing some of the techniques her father had taught her, and she had never been more grateful for the knowledge of them. "Mother, Wilson and I are very serious. We love each other. We've gotten close. He has even been talking about marriage with me, and he said he wants to discuss it with you and Daddy."

Kimiko's head snapped back to face Jillian and her eyes and lips narrowed into needle thin lines. "How dare you speak about anything like that to a vagrant like that boy! I can't even believe you refer to him as your boyfriend! He is no such thing! He does not have my permission nor your father's to be in that kind of a relationship with you. He comes from a poor and broken family and he has absolutely no prospects for his future. If I had realized that you were taking him this seriously, I would have forbidden you to see him.

"You have been raised far better than to honestly think you could be anything more than acquaintances with a little gutter tramp like that! I'm shocked. I'm outraged! Marriage. Don't you even consider dating anyone, let alone speaking to anyone about marriage unless your father and I have already approved of it! Think of the dishonor you would bring this family! Think of the dishonor you would bring to our name! I cannot believe you would do such a thing!" Kimiko placed her hands flat on the table and glared at her daughter.

"I forbid you to see him or speak with him ever again. You will not act in such a haphazard way. You know we must approve of any young man interested in you, and you will not date or marry anyone that I have not chosen for you. Do not dare to defy your parents, your family or your culture. You owe us everything. Do you hear me? *Everything.* You will date who I allow you to date, and I am telling you right now that you will date Carter's son, and there will be no discussion about it."

Jillian tried to keep all of her emotions in. She knew she must not treat her mother with disrespect. "Please don't make my life part of your business dealings, Mother. Our family's company is doing fine without Mr. Carter. If you want to do business with him, then do business with him, but my life shouldn't have any bearing on it, and the marriage I enter into should be for love, not for money."

Kimiko scoffed again. "You know so little. You are young and you cannot see into the future like I can. You are thinking with a child's mind and a child's heart and it will make a fool of you and of all of us." She leaned slightly toward Jillian. "Think, my daughter, think carefully. Who will inherit our family's business here in the states? Who will run it? You will. You have an obligation to your family and a responsibility to the business that your uncles in Japan have worked so hard to build up. You would throw all of that away for some idiotic romantic notions you are too young to understand? I won't hear of it. The wise move is to align you with a family who can help our business grow into the future, not with someone who will bring no honor to our family nor benefit to your life. Carter's son carries a good strong name and he is from a family wealthier than ours. His father has a thriving business that could one day be merged with ours.

"More good business opportunities could be achieved if the families are close. This is your duty to all of your family. We have technological advances in Japan that have no equal in the world, and Carter is interested in them.

"You and his son could carry those advances into the future and be the foundation of the technological world to come. Look beyond your ridiculous childhood fantasies and focus on the future, make your family a priority and uphold your obligation and duty to all of us. Do not even consider shaming or dishonoring us by going against my instructions."

Jillian heard the words coming at her like hail stones in a freezing blizzard that she could not escape. Honor. Dignity. Respect. Tradition. Obligation. Responsibility. Family. Business. She felt as though her mother's hands were so enormous that they could fit around her whole body and squeeze until Jillian had no room to think or breathe or live at all. She knew there was no way out of it. She knew she could not go against her mother's wishes. Her heart felt like every bit of light in it had been squeezed out and there was nothing left but the outer skin of it.

She looked straight forward as her mother spoke on, but she didn't hear the words her mother spoke. She was thinking of Wilson. She thought of how much she loved him and how much he loved her. She thought of how he had gone on and on talking with her about marriage and their life together. She knew he had nothing to offer her but his love, and she believed that would be enough. Jillian thought of stories she knew in which the lovers ran away together, but she knew that she could never desert her family. She could never leave.

She realized that her mother and father had never actually spent time with Wilson. They'd only met him at the house on a few occasions when he was coming by to pick Jillian up to go out. The tiniest sliver of hope began to glow within her. Perhaps if they got to know him better, perhaps if they spent some time with him, they would see what a good and loving young man he was and then they would realize that it would be a good match for her to be with him. The hope of it lifted her spirits a bit and she determined that she would try to make it happen before she had to meet Carter's son.

27

Kimiko picked up her purse and looked through it, then set it back down on the seat beside her. "I've left my cell phone in the car. Let me use yours so that I can call your father."

Jillian reached into her purse and then handed her cell phone to her mother who excused herself from the table and disappeared. She took the welcome solitude to take a deep breath and try to relax her body from the shock and hurt she had just experienced.

How could her mother try to make her date a man she didn't know or care about? She disliked the boy intensely from the incident they had experienced when she was a child and now her mother wanted her to date him! It was unthinkable! She would just have to bring Wilson to the house to have him spend time with her parents so that they could see how wonderful he really was. He would change their minds. They would see. Then she would be able to be with him and marry him.

Her mother was gone for a long while, but eventually she returned and silently handed Jillian her phone and took her seat again.

"Carter is going to have his son call you. Be ready for the call, be polite and friendly to him, and if he asks you out on a date, go with him. Do you understand?" she asked pointedly. Jillian took a deep breath. She was going to have to work fast. "I understand," she said quietly.

They finished their tea and drove home. Kimiko disappeared into her office and Jillian walked to the garden and sat on her favorite bench beside the koi pond, underneath a weeping willow tree. She pulled her phone from her bag and called Wilson.

It rang several times, but finally, he answered.

"Hello?" he said in a sullen voice.

"Hi, it's me," she said, a smile spreading over her face as his voice sounded in her ear and reverberated through her heart.

28

"Hi."

"I was thinking that it would be good if you got to know my parents better. They haven't really spent any time with you and they don't know you very well. They're kind of protective of me. I want you to come over for dinner tonight so you can talk with them and let them become more familiar with you. Can you come please?" she asked, all her hope beginning to soar.

There was a long quiet moment and then Wilson said softly, "Jillian, there's something I need to tell you."

It didn't sound good. She had talked with him that morning and he had been fine; he had sounded happy and in love, but now he only sounded empty. "Oh no, what is it? What's wrong?" she asked, concern swelling in her.

He sighed audibly. "I don't think we should see each other anymore." His voice remained low.

Jillian's heart stopped mid-beat. "Wha...What?" she stammered.

"I don't think we should see each other anymore," he repeated a little louder.

"What are you talking about?" she whispered, as everything in her began to spin like a cyclone; her thoughts and feelings whirring about her out of control.

"Well, I didn't know how to tell you this, but there's this other girl I met, and I've kind of been seeing her on the side, I guess. She's uh... she kind of wants to get serious with me, and I want that with her, too." He stumbled through the words.

Jillian felt like lightning was cracking through her head and heart, and her soul was being ripped in half. Tears stung her eyes and blinded her, spilling out onto her face in streams. Her voice was suddenly gone and it cracked when she tried to speak.

"What are you talking about, Wilson? We were talking about getting married this morning! What other girl?"

He sounded miserable. "Just another girl. You don't know her. You don't need to know her. I really think I'm falling in love with her, to tell you the truth. She's prettier than you, she's sweeter than you, and she lives in my neighborhood; she isn't a richie like you are. I don't feel like I have to live up to her lifestyle when I'm with her. Listen, I know we were talking about getting married and all that, but I didn't really mean it. I don't feel like I'm good enough for you and I never will be, so I think it's best if we just call everything off right now, okay?"

She choked on a sob and trembled as she held the phone against her ear, her eyes shut tight, trying to hold in the riptide of pain that was coursing through her. "How could you?" she whispered. "I love you!"

He was quiet as she began to sob. Her chest heaved with the weight of her broken heart and sorrow, and she covered her face with her hand, sliding down off the bench onto the grass beside the pond and laying on her side.

Wilson did not cry, but his breath grew very short and raspy. "Listen, I gotta go. Don't call me anymore, okay? Just… just go live your life and be happy. I'm glad I had you while I did. I'll miss you," he said quietly.

She didn't hear him hang up as she sobbed into her hands and arms, lying on the grass. Her phone shut itself off and it seemed like an eternity before she felt a large warm hand on her back.

"Baby, what's wrong? Why are you crying? What happened?" her father asked her. She had cried so hard that her face was swollen and her eyes were red. She rolled over slowly and let her daddy pick her up into his arms. He held her and rocked her back and forth, and then he reached up and wiped her tears away.

"Come on now, it's going to be alright. There's nothing we can't fix. Come on, baby, tell me what happened. What's got you so upset?" His voice was low and soft and it soothed her, like it always had.

"Everything," she whispered and then looked up at him through her soaked eyelashes. "Wilson and I just broke up. He said he found another girl! Daddy, we were talking just this morning about getting married! How could he do that?" She began to cry again.

Samson rocked her back and forth some more and held her to the solid wall of his chest. "It's alright baby girl. It's alright. Boys don't make the best decisions sometimes, and if he let you go, well that's the most foolish thing he could have done, but it only means that you have a chance to find someone better; someone who will really love you, and that's the best thing you can hope for, honey."

She looked up at him again with irritation on her beautiful face. "Daddy! Do you know that Mother told me today that I have to date some stranger? She said she has this old business acquaintance that has a son and she wants me to go out with him and date him so that our families can do better business! It's awful! Did you know about that?" she asked, searching her father's eyes.

He closed his eyes for a moment and nodded. "I did know about that. She talked with me about it. I'll say this, baby girl, sometimes, especially when we are young, we can't see as well or as far as those who are older and wiser than us can see, and oftentimes when we are young, we are ruled by our hearts more frequently than our minds, and it can lead to trouble. She's not trying to hurt you, baby, she would never do that. She wants what's best for you, just like I do, and she thinks maybe he might be a good boy for you to spend some time with."

Jillian felt crushed beneath all her grief, but she always listened to her father. "Daddy," she said quietly and sniffed, "do you want me to go out with him?"

Samson looked away for a moment and then looked back at her. "I want you to be happy. It looks to me like that boy Wilson didn't make you very happy. Maybe you could do your old dad a big favor and keep some peace in this house, and just this once go out with the new boy, just so things settle down with your mother. If you don't like him later on after you've given him a chance, why then let him go, but then you can say that you gave it a try, and that will show obedience to your mother. What do you say, baby girl?"

Jillian felt like nothing was worth talking about anymore, and her own choices had led her to an obliterated heart, so she might as well heed the words of the wisest man she knew.
"Alright, Daddy. I'll go out with him. I'm not going to like it, but I'll do it," she said stubbornly, remembering with bitterness how the boy had left her among the shards of jade on the ground.

"That's my girl," Samson said, brushing his hand over her hair and kissing her forehead. "Thank you, Jillian. Now, let's go get you some tea to calm you down and take some of that heartache away. I have just the thing."

She sniffed again. "Is there ginger in it?" she asked hopefully.

He nodded and pulled her to her feet. "Of course there is." He smiled and walked her to his dojo with his arm around her shoulder.

Chapter 3

Reed was lounging in the sun by the enormous sea shell shaped pool behind the house, sulking about the date his father was forcing him to go on. It wasn't the worst thing his father had ever made him do though, so he knew it could be worse. He picked up his phone and dialed the number his father had given him.

It rang a few times and a pleasant female voice answered.

"Hello?"

"Hello. I wonder if I might speak with Jillian?" he smiled so that he would sound as pleasant as she did, though he certainly wasn't feeling it.

"This is Jillian."

"Jillian, this is Reed. Our parents suggested that we might spend some time together, so I thought I would call you and invite you to dinner tonight," he said, holding his smile in place.

"That would be lovely, thank you." she said mechanically, but politely.

"Shall I come by your house around six?" he asked, smile intact.

"Six is perfect. I'll see you then," she answered. "Thank you, Reed."

"Of course. I'll see you then. Good-bye," he said and hung up, unscrewing the smile from his face and pushing his sunglasses back up on his nose. He laid his head back and relaxed in the sunshine, and fell asleep.

Jillian hung up the phone and fell back on her bed, looking at the ceiling in her room. She was not at all excited about their dinner date. She was still nursing her seriously broken heart. Her mother knocked on the paper screened door to her bedroom.

"Yes?" she called out, not moving.

"Was that Carter's son?" her mother asked in a loud voice.

"Yes."

"You made a date with him?" her mother continued.

"Yes. Dinner tonight." She tried not to sound sullen.
"Good. Make a good impression so that you will be going out again after tonight," her mother intoned seriously.

"Yes, Mother," Jillian replied, closing her eyes and hating her life.

Later that evening she was flipping through her closet wondering what to wear and finally settled on a sleeveless, tea-length, sky blue, chiffon dress with a sweetheart neckline. It was subtly form fitting without being revealing and slightly demure without being frumpy. She picked up some high heels and her cardigan in case she got cool later that evening. Jillian was just slipping silver earrings in her ears when her father knocked on her door.

"Come in," she called out.

He slid her screen door open and stepped inside. "Don't you look pretty!" he said, smiling. He walked up to her and hugged her, looking into her mirror with her. "My girl is the prettiest in the world."

She smiled and hugged him back tightly. "Thank you, Daddy."

"He's here, baby girl. He seems nice," he said softly. "I think it will be an enjoyable evening for you."

She looked up at him with some gratitude. "That's good to know, Daddy."

He walked her to the foyer and as she rounded the corner, she saw him. He was incredibly good looking. Dark wavy hair slightly tousled and mostly tamed back, bright blue eyes and a wide brilliant smile. He was tall and muscular; the curves of his arms and his chest were not hidden by the fine dinner jacket he was wearing. He was talking to her mother, who was smiling happily at him, and he turned to look at her just as her eyes had finished appraising him.

She saw the expression on his face change. She saw that same look on many people's faces when they saw her; she was so unusual that her beauty often caught people off guard and she was used to double takes and staring. She was all too familiar with the way his eyes opened a bit wider and his mouth opened slightly in a partial gape and then curved into a grin. She saw his eyes as they flickered down her body and then held her eyes again.

"Well hello, you must be Jillian!" he said in pleasant surprise. He was surprised. She looked different than he had remembered. He knew her parents were watching him, particularly her father who was walking behind her as she came toward him, so he didn't get the leisurely gaze over her body that a quick glance at her told him he wanted to have.

That one glance had suggested that she had curves he wanted to spend quite a bit of time
looking at, or possibly undressing. His heart began to beat faster as he gazed at her face. She had stunning features; a fine boned facial structure, dark golden skin like chocolate covered in honey, and her hair… it was pulled up into a loose bun on her head, but wisps of it fell around her beautiful face, framing it, drawing his attention to her big dark eyes and her full lips. She smiled politely at him and he snapped back to the moment at hand.

"I'm Reed. It's wonderful to meet you again. You look quite lovely this evening." He bowed to her and took her hand lightly in his, brushing his lips over the back of her hand for a brief moment before letting it go and turning toward her mother.

"I brought this gift from my father with his best wishes." He bowed and handed a beautifully decorated bottle of sake to Kimiko.

She bowed in return. "Thank you, Reed. Please tell your father that was very kind of him and we are humbled by his thoughtfulness and generosity."

Samson placed his hand on Jillian's shoulder. "Where will you be taking my baby girl tonight?" he asked seriously, his eyes holding Reed's sternly.

"We'll be having dinner at the Carlton tonight. I promise not to keep her out too late," he said with a gleaming smile.

Kimiko nodded. "Please don't worry about keeping her too late. Take your time and enjoy yourself," she said with a smile. Jillian looked sharply at her. She suddenly felt like she was being sold off to the highest bidder.

"Take good care of my baby girl," Samson said, his eyes still trained on Reed.

"Yes, sir, of course," Reed answered with a nod and smile. He held out his arm and Jillian slipped her hand loosely around his elbow and he led her out the door. Her parents both watched her go, and as she turned to look over her shoulder at them, she noticed that they had very different expressions on their faces. Her mother looked extremely pleased with herself and her father looked reticent.

Reed opened the door of his red Ferrari and she raised her eyebrows and sighed as he helped her into the car and closed the door behind her. When he closed his own door and put his seatbelt on, he turned toward her slightly as though he needed to find the belt latch, which allowed him to get a better look at the woman next to him. His eyes lingered over the voluptuous curve of her breasts, her narrow waist and the roundness of her hips.

"That's a pretty dress. It does a lot to bring out that gorgeous body of yours, but you might want to wear clothes that show a little more… skin…" he said as he drank in the sight of her.

She was horrified. "Reed! How could you say something like that? You just met me!" she huffed at him. "That's so disrespectful!" He zipped down the road and looked over his arm at her. "How is that disrespectful? It's a compliment. You're a beautiful woman. You have a gorgeous body. Women who don't have gorgeous bodies would probably love to hear a man say something like that to them. Don't scorn the compliment just because it isn't packaged all neatly with a polite bow.

"I'm saying you are one beautiful lady, and most women would kill to look like you. You should show it off a little more instead of hiding all that beauty under so much clothing. You're wearing too much. You have an incredible body. Show it off. What's insulting about that?"

She glared at him. "It's disrespectful of you to comment on my body at all. First of all, it's not your business what I wear or how I display my body if I even display it all. I choose my clothes to suit my style and personality and no one else's. I didn't wake up this morning and think, 'oh… I wonder what Reed would like to see me in… I wonder what Reed would want for me to wear… I wonder what would make Reed happy…' No. I wear what I like and what I want.

"I happen to think this is a pretty dress and I think I look pretty in it, and that's it. I don't really care what you think or want, so kindly keep your opinions to yourself." Then she turned and looked out of the window.

Reed was unaccustomed to women talking to him that way, or anyone else, for that matter. He was used to having the world handed to him on a silver platter by everyone but his father. He wasn't quite sure how to respond to it.

He sighed. "I think we got off on the wrong foot. I'm sorry. I just wanted to tell you that you look beautiful."

She realized that she was being defensive because this was a forced date and she was giving him too hard a time. Guilt began to bite at her and she, too, sighed. "I'm sorry. I didn't mean to snap at you. Thank you for the compliment, but perhaps if you're going to say something like that to a woman, give it a little thought first and make it sound more polite."

He shook his head. "I don't know what's impolite about telling you I really like the way you look, but okay," he said, shrugging his shoulders. They drove to the restaurant in silence the rest of the way, but he kept stealing glances at her legs every chance he got and she noticed but didn't say anything to him about it.

They were seated immediately at the restaurant and she was impressed by the attentive service they received.

Reed took every opportunity he could to look at Jillian from every angle as they had gotten out of the car, headed into the restaurant, were seated and then finally he could face her. He still wasn't finished looking at her. She was finished with him looking at her, though.
"You must hear this often, but you really are stunning. You have such a unique look about you," he said with a lazy grin, staring at her face.

"Most people don't actually vocalize it," she replied with a salty tone.

"What do they do, just stare at you?" he asked, wondering aloud.

"Have you decided what you want to eat?" she asked, changing the topic and holding his menu out to him.

"I know what I want," he said, grinning at her and smiling in a suggestive way.

"You should look at the menu. They might not be offering what you want," she retorted.

He chuckled and took the menu from her hands. "Sassy. I like it!" he said, the corners of his mouth curled upward.

She ignored him. She was so irritated with him already. He was acting like a horny teenager, staring at her and making comments about her body. This was who her parents wanted her to date?

They ordered their meals and he decided he had better play it safe with her until he could figure her out. She was acting cooler than most girls he talked to. Actually, she was acting cooler than all the girls he talked to. No woman had ever ignored him; as a matter of fact, they regularly fell all over him and swooned if he paid any attention to them at all. This one seemed annoyed with him. It hadn't ever happened before.

"I guess we met before when we were kids," he said with a more polite tone. "Do you remember that? It was a long time ago; I'd be surprised if you did."

"Surprise, I do," she said shortly.

He was caught off guard and he stopped momentarily, lifting his drink and taking a long pull off of it before he set it back down.

"That was an unfortunate event," he said a bit more quietly.

"It was unfortunate for you," she said, her eyes glued to the wine menu. She wasn't reading it, but she didn't want to look at him.

"I can't imagine it was a pleasant experience for you," he replied.

"It was one of the worst experiences of my childhood and I don't care to discuss it further or ever," she said and then waved at the waiter, and asked him for a glass of wine.

Reed was stopped short again. He took another drink and felt uncertain about what else to say to her, but luckily, that's when the

39

meal was brought to their table and he was glad to have an excuse to keep his mouth closed.

They talked lightly throughout dinner about the weather and the restaurant, their food and the service where they were. Reed couldn't help himself, and he continued to look at Jillian's body and face all throughout the meal. Jillian tried her best not to look at him, as she felt it was gracing him with far too much of her attention and that was what he wanted more than anything, just like when they were children.

They finished the meal and Reed got her back into the car. He stole sidelong glances at her and decided that he wasn't through with her for the evening, though she didn't say anything to him about continuing their time together or going back to her house.

He thought he would take her for a drive, so he wound his car slowly up into the hills for a while before she finally turned to look straight at him. "Where are we going?" she asked.

He looked back at her and smiled. "I thought we might go for a drive. We can head up to the hills and see a sunset together. It might be nice to enjoy with each other. I realize our parents are the ones who want us to spend time with one another, but it could still be enjoyable if we make it that way," he said with an earnest smile at her.

She suddenly felt a huge wave of guilt. "I'm sorry. I haven't really been giving you a chance at all. I'm still holding a bit of a grudge from the incident when we were children and I'm not thrilled that my mother wants me to date you… and that has nothing to do with you, it has more to do with being allowed to make my own choices."

He pulled the car onto a deserted stretch of land that looked over the city down below and they could see the sun setting into the ocean. He helped her out of the car and they went and stood in front of it and looked out at the view.

"To be honest, I wasn't really thrilled about it either, when my father brought it up, but I will say that I have done my best to give you a fun evening and I don't seem to be making a good impression with you." He turned toward her slightly, his hands in his pockets and he let his eyes wander up her legs and slowly take in every curve on her body until he reached her face, which was still pointed toward the sunset.

"I understand. I really haven't been very fair to you." she replied, and her mother's words rang through her mind… 'make a good impression'…. "I am sorry about that," she said, looking down and then turning to look up at him with an apologetic expression.

Before she knew it, Reed had slipped his hands from his pockets and reached for her face, tilting it upward to meet his. He pressed his lips against hers gently, softly at first and then he opened her mouth with his and kissed her deeply. Her hands flew up to his shoulders and she pressed against them to push him away, but Reed held her head firmly with one hand and slid his other hand over her breast, squeezing it and then he reached around behind her and grasped her rounded hip, pressing her snugly to him.

He moaned in pleasure and she jerked her face away from his, finally breaking his grasp on her head, but not escaping his arm around her or his hand clamped to her hip.

"What do you think you're doing?!" she yelled at him in disgust.

He smiled at her, pulling her close to him and he leaned in and kissed her neck softly, just beneath her ear. "I'm letting you make it up to me. You've behaved like a stuck up snob all night and now you say you're sorry. Well, this is how I'm going to let you make it up to me." He trailed warm, soft wet kisses down her neck. "Besides, honey, this is what our parents want. I'm just doing what you and I are expected to do." He reached for her head again and planted his mouth over hers, kissing her deeply again.

Guilt and fury wrestled within Jillian as he dominated her mouth and sent sparks of electricity shooting through her body. She didn't want anything like this to happen between them, but he was right, this was exactly what her mother wanted, and the woman would have been pleased to know that Reed liked her and wanted her, but at the same time, she was outraged that no one was respecting her feelings or her desires and wishes; not her mother, not Carter, and certainly not Reed.

He reached his other hand around her so that both of them were firmly grasping the fullness of her hips while he kissed her, his tongue sweeping over hers hungrily, and he pulled her tightly to his hips, pressing his rock solid erection against her and rubbing the bulge of it against her inner thigh. Flames of desire shot through him and he groaned in need as the feel of her body against his filled him with lust for her.

She couldn't stand another moment of him, and his advances had finally gone much too far. She wriggled out of his grasp and moved several steps away from him.

"Our parents might want this," she said breathlessly, trying to slow her anger and her heart, "but I sure as hell don't! You have no business whatsoever treating me like that! Did I ask you to kiss me? No!

"Did I invite you to feel me up or start grinding on me? No! What is it with you? Do you think you can just do whatever you want with any woman at all and she just has to go along with it? Do you think I'm standing here for nothing more than your physical pleasure? Well, I'm not! You need to get a grip!" she yelled at him.

He stood before her, staring at her in absolute shock, and complete arousal. No woman had ever told him no or not wanted him before. It was a totally foreign experience to him.

"I had a grip…" he teased, smiling at her and stepping toward her. "I had a great grip, but you broke out of it. What is it with you? What's your big hang up, anyway? I tell you how gorgeous you are, and you get insulted.

"I try to flirt a little and you shut me down. I bring you up here to enjoy the sunset and you apologize to me for acting so cold and mean, and then when I give you a little kiss, you freak out and get all upset!" He stepped closer to her again.

"That was not a little kiss!" she snapped at him. "Your hands were all over me!"

He chuckled and nodded slightly. "Oh yeah, honey, that was indeed just a little kiss. If you want, I can give you a really good kiss," he stepped toward her again and she held her ground, "a kiss that will make you melt right in my arms, and you will feel things that you have never felt before." He grinned at her and she glared at him. He paused in his approach toward her.

"Hey, are you sorry or not? Are you interested in making this a good date or not? Come on. Come here and make it up to me. Be a good girl." He reached for her and closed his hands around her waist, pulling her to him again, looking directly into her eyes. "This is what our parents want," he said with slight sarcasm. "Let's give them what they want. We can't be disobedient." He threw the statement at her and it hit her squarely in the heart.

She froze. Was she being disobedient? Her mother had been so adamant about her being with Reed. Her heart began to pound and she felt a little panic rise in her. Reed reached up and slipped the comb from her hair and it tumbled down her back and over her shoulders, falling all around her like a satin curtain. He stared at it, and stared at her.

"Holy sh…" he started to say and stopped himself. His voice came out in a reverent whisper. "You look unbelievable…" He barely spoke the words.

As if in a trance, he reached one hand up and touched her hair, letting his fingers glide over it slowly and weave into the strands as he lowered his hand. Then he cupped her face with that hand, her hair still twined into his fingers, and with his other hand on her back, pulled her toward him and pressed his lips against hers, tasting her more slowly this time, sucking gently on her full lips and her tongue, discovering her mouth with his and losing himself in the exotic sensuality of her. "You are so delicious…" he said in a soft voice, his lips barely leaving hers as he spoke, his heart pounding heavy in his chest.

She fought against the internal battle between the obedience she knew she owed to her mother and the independence she wanted so desperately to have for herself. She tried to deny it with everything in her, but Reed's kiss was sending very hot waves through her body and she wished desperately that her body wasn't betraying her just then, and that it would be as repulsed by him as her brain was. It was then that she felt his hand close over her breast again and begin to massage it, squeezing it as his thumb moved over her hardening nipple. That was all she could stand.

Reed was so enraptured in his passionate moment that the sound and feel of her hand as it smacked his face was a complete shock to him. Added to that was the fact that no woman had ever hit him or denied him anything he wanted. He stumbled back from her in amazement and shock, his hand on his face and everything in him swirling in chaos and confusion. The physical sting of her slap was painful, but it was nothing compared to the jarring impact on his ego.

"What the hell was that for?" he asked, completely incensed at her rejection of his advances.

"Just who do you think you are?!" she yelled at him again. "I just told you that you had no business doing that to me! We don't even know each other! How can you be like that with someone you just met! You're so disgusting!"

He was completely stunned. "…disgusting?" He felt a rare anger rise up in him. "You think you're the only one who was told to go on this date? You aren't! I didn't want to be here either, but here I am, doing what is expected of me, and you go off half cocked and hit me! What the hell are *you* thinking?"

She was outraged. "How dare you! What makes you think you have the right to touch anyone like that without being invited to do it? I didn't even kiss you back! You're unbelievable!"

"Oh you think that was the wrong move on my part? You seemed to like it just fine by the feel of it!" he spat back at her, nodding at her breasts. Her nipples were stiffened and straining against the sky blue material. She cursed them silently and yelled at him.

"All of your moves have been wrong right from the start, when we were kids! Take me home right now! I don't want anything to do with you! Nothing! What a pig you are!" she yelled and then turned on her heel and got back into the car, slamming the door behind her and glaring out her window so she wouldn't have to look at him.

He got into the car as well and zoomed quickly back down the mountain, clenching his teeth in anger. He pulled up to her house and she jumped out of his car and slammed the door shut again. He was gone down the road before she had taken two steps.

Hot tears stung her eyes and she covered her mouth, looking up at the front door of the house in dismay. She knew her mother would want the details of her date, and she had no idea how she was going to explain it. She trembled and tried to take deep breaths to calm herself, and she quietly let herself into the house. Her father was sitting in a chair in the front room, a lamp on beside him and a book in his hand. His eyes went straight to her when she walked in and he immediately set the book down and walked to her.

 Samson enveloped her in a big warm hug and she finally let silent tears stream from her eyes and roll down her cheeks. She held her breath so that she would not sob and draw her mother's attention. She didn't see her mother in the room and she didn't want to. Jillian looked up at her father and he touched his finger to his lips, indicating that they should be quiet.

He led her out of the back of the house, through the garden and into his dojo. As soon as the screen closed behind her and they were alone, she let the sobs out and he held her as she cried in frustration, anger, and sorrow.

He didn't say a word to her until she calmed down and he dried the tears from her face. "Well," he said softly, "I guess it didn't go as nicely as we had hoped?"

"He was horrible Daddy! He's a disgusting pig and I don't want anything to do with him." She wept miserably.

Her father looked stern. "Did he hurt you?" he asked.

"He didn't hurt me. He was unbelievably disrespectful, but I'm not hurt," she said through her tears.

Her dad held her close again and rubbed her back. "It's alright, baby. It's alright."

"Daddy, Mother wants me to date him. She told me to make a good impression on him so he'd want to see me again and I didn't!" She looked up at him in consternation.

He smiled down at her. "Oh now, you're a good girl, Jillian. I'm sure it wasn't that bad. What could you have done that would drive him so far away that he wouldn't want to see you again?"

She spoke quietly. "I slapped his face."

Samson raised one eyebrow. "You slapped his face? Well, if he pushed you that far, I know he must have deserved it. Don't you think about it any longer, baby girl. You're home and you are alright. Let it go, now."

"Mother is going to be furious if she finds out," Jillian said, her eyes falling to her hands that were folded in her lap.

"Well, just don't tell her that part. I'm proud of you anyway. I'm glad you think enough of yourself to stop a man when he goes too far." Samson smiled at her. "You're a strong woman. It's one of your best traits. You know you get that from your mother," he said with a wink and a smile.

Jillian rolled her eyes and sighed, letting out the last of her grief from the evening. She had cried herself tired. "Well, I'm going to sneak off to bed so I don't have to talk to her about it until tomorrow. Maybe I'll dream up a good story tonight that I can tell her later. She just doesn't understand me! You're the only one who really gets me, Daddy. You're the only one who is even a little bit like me." She reached over and set her hand beside his, looking at the comparison between the two of them. Matching skin. Matching people. Her team.

"Baby girl, I am leaving early in the morning." Her dad looked at her with sorrowful eyes.

She sat up and looked at him in surprise. "Leaving? Where are you going?"

"Your uncles in Japan need me there to help them with the business for a little while, so I'm going to go give them a hand," he admitted to her.

She shook her head in denial. "No! Daddy don't leave me here! Take me with you!"

"I'm sorry, my girl, but this is a long trip and you need to stay here at home." He patted her back. "I'll call you and check in on you. I promise," he said with a half smile.

Jillian was back to being miserable. "How long will you be gone?" she asked in a whisper.

"A month," he answered quietly.

She lowered her head sadly and laid it against his shoulder. "I'm going to miss you so much, Daddy." Her voice wavered.

"I'm going to miss you, too, baby girl."

Chapter4

Reed walked into the dining room the morning after his disaster date and his father didn't even bother to greet him with a 'good morning'.

"How did it go last night?" Carter asked immediately.

Reed sagged down into his seat and picked up his coffee cup. "It was terrible."

Carter's gaze hardened. "What do you mean it was terrible? What happened?"

"She's a snob and a goody-two shoes. It was a rotten night." Reed stabbed at his breakfast with his fork.

Carter leaned toward his son and glared at him. "Please tell me you didn't try to make a move on that girl. She's a conservative girl from a traditional Japanese family and she isn't like one of your little play things. She's a lady. What did you do to her?" Carter demanded.

Reed grew defensive. "Nothing! Carter, nothing happened. I just don't like her."

Carter drew a deep breath and let it out slowly. "Well, son, that's too bad."

"Why is that?" Reed asked as suspicion built in his mind.

"Because you're going to ask her to marry you."

Reed almost jumped out of his chair. "*What?!*" he shouted.

Carter looked at him with an unwavering gaze. "You are going to ask that girl to marry you, immediately. If you don't ask her to marry you, I'm going to give the company to your younger brother and you are going to be disinherited. You will lose your car. You will be kicked out of this house permanently. You will have no money whatsoever to go and make a new life. You will be barred from ever returning, and you will not have any place in my life again."

Reed was too stunned to speak.

Carter continued. "You have driven me too far, Reed. You are an embarrassment to this family and to the company that I have worked so hard all of my life to build. You go through women and money like they are running water. You have done nothing to improve your life or yourself, and you have no future ahead of you.

"I refuse to continue to contribute to your lifestyle or the impending demise of my home, this family's reputation or my company because you have chosen to be a careless playboy. This is your one and only chance, and you know I am dead serious about this. You marry that girl and make a solid responsible life for yourself or you are out of here. I want an engagement ring on her hand within the week."

Reed stared at his father. He knew Carter was deadly serious. He also remembered quite vividly, the sting of the slap she had planted on his cheek the night before and her insistence that she never wanted to see him again.

"I'm not so sure that Jillian likes me very much. What if I got engaged to another girl?" Reed offered weakly, trying to compromise with his father.

Carter held his gaze on his son. "You will marry Jillian. It's your problem and your fault if she doesn't like you. You figure it out. You have one week. Get a ring on her hand."

Reed sat back in his chair and felt chaos and disbelief flooding through him. He was going to lose his whole life. He was going to lose his home and his family. He was going to lose everything, because he had been too hot handed the night before and let his hormones get the better of him like they always did. There was no way she was going to even agree to see him, let alone allow him to try to talk her into marrying him.

The idea of marriage terrified him. It was a lifelong commitment to one woman. He could not see the appeal of it at all, except for the fact that everything he had, everything that meant anything to him would be gone forever if he didn't get engaged to a woman who hated him, and he had less than a week to do it. Hercules never faced a tougher task than the one that was looming over Reed.

He stood up and left his breakfast on the table, shoving his hands down into the depths of his pockets. He looked at his father and let out a deep sigh. "No problem, Carter," he said shortly, and turned and walked out of the dining room.

Reed headed to his brother's office which was near his father's. He was grateful to see the young man sitting at his desk when he walked in and closed the door.

"Hey, Anderson," he said quietly and lowered himself into a chair in front of his brother's desk.

His brother turned to look at him. "Hi, Reed." He looked at him carefully and leaned back in his chair. "Dad must have talked to you."

"Yeah, he did," Reed said with a sigh. "Listen… Andy, if by some chance you wind up getting… everything…. Would you cut me out of it all? Would you leave me hanging out in the wind like Carter was saying? Or would you look after your big brother and maybe give me a job or something?"
Anderson shook his head. "A job? You mean a handout. Listen, Reed, you're my brother and I love you plenty, but you've done a lot of damage here and at the company, and I've had to clean up a lot of the messes you've left. You think dad goes in and takes care of it all? No way, Reed. He always dumps it in my lap and I get to deal with it.

"I'm on a first name basis with most of the elite businesses around town because I'm constantly on the phone with them sending them checks to pay for the havoc you wreak."

Reed sank down in the chair.

"Besides, the old man had the lawyers draw it up so that no one in the family or the business can lend you a hand, or a handout. You're on your own for real if you don't tie the knot with that girl. I wouldn't worry about it too much, though, Reed. After all, you're the ladies' man. Didn't she fall in love with you the minute she laid eyes on you? How did it go?" Anderson asked, tilting his head and raising his eyebrow.

Reed leaned forward and covered his face with his hands. "She hates me."

Anderson leaned forward in his chair and stared at his brother in shock. "She hates you? How could she hate you? No women hate you!"

Reed raised his head and rested his chin in his hand. "She is the exception to the rule, of course. Trust me when I tell you, you probably better plan on getting everything. Let's have dinner before the end of the week. I'm going to miss you, little brother."

Anderson gaped. "No way…. No way!" He almost laughed just a little, but it turned into a frown. "How…?"

"I'm asking myself the same question, Andy." He stood up. "Well, I'll see you soon for dinner, brother. Bye." Reed walked out of his brother's office and headed for his car, pulling out his cell phone as he closed the car door behind him.

It rang once and she answered. "Hey, baby!" Excitement poured through the phone and made him smile a little.

"Hi, Daisy. Listen, are you busy? I'm going to spend the afternoon and probably the night on my father's yacht in the marina with a very old bottle of booze. Care to come to the boat and join me?" he asked, hoping for some sympathy.

"Um, well I'm supposed to dance at the club tonight, but I'll see if I can get one of the other girls to take my show." Daisy sounded uncertain.

"Oh... well, if you're busy I can find someone else who has the time to..." he started to drawl. He felt like being mean to someone, anyone, just to bleed some of the poison from himself that had been building all morning.
"Oh, no! Baby, don't do that. I'll be there. Don't you worry. I'll be there as soon as I can." She jumped right into his sentence, reassuring him.

"Okay. See you soon," he said and hung up.

Two hours later he was lying on the deck of the boat, sunglasses on, bottle of scotch half empty and hanging from his hand when she strolled over to him and sat on the deck chair beside him.

"Hi, baby." She grinned down at him.

"Hey," he said, opening his eyes and looking over at her. She was in a skimpy bikini and it was barely covered by a white tie-front shirt. He laid his head back, his eyes feasting on her body. "I'm so glad you're here. I need you to make me feel better."

She grinned and leaned over to him, kissing him softly and slowly for a long moment before running her hands over his bare chest.

"What do you want, baby?" she asked with a happy smile.

He pulled her on top of him and wrapped his arms around her. "Everything. I want everything."

"You got it." She pressed her soft pink lips to his, running the tip of her tongue over them and then taking her sweet time to taste his mouth. She felt his erection grow beneath her body and she giggled happily and reached her hand down to rub the stiffness of it over his shorts.

He arched his back and moaned. "Come on, let's go downstairs. I don't need anymore bad publicity." He sat up slowly and they walked down the steps into the center of the yacht. He took her to the master cabin and slowly began to untie her cover shirt, slipping it from her shoulders as he kissed her breasts, one at a time, and then he let the shirt fall to the floor.

She stared at him for a moment and then closed her eyes and let him do whatever he wanted. He tugged at the strings of her bikini and it too fell away from her body easily, and in moments she was standing before him nude. She pulled his shorts off and ran her hands up his arms, resting them on his shoulders.

Reed lifted his hands to her large round breasts and stroked her hard pink nipples. She'd paid a lot of money for her breasts to look the way they did, and she believed it had been worth every dime. He squeezed and massaged them, cupped them and rubbed them.

"What's all this about, baby?" She opened her eyes and studied his face. He didn't look at her, he just studied her body as though he was sealing it into his memory forever.

"Shhhh." He hushed her, and moved his hands down over her belly and her hips, then lifted her and laid her back on the bed. She closed her eyes and smiled. Reed took his time running his hands over her legs and then he took a long swig from the bottle of scotch he'd brought with him and offered some to her. She drank. He put the cap back on the bottle and set it close to them on the bed.

"Why are you always around, Daisy?" he asked, running his fingers over the soft triangle of blonde hair beneath her belly and stroking the core of her. "You're always there when I need you. Why do you do that?" he asked, looking at her face.

"Do you really want to know?" she asked, knowing that it should never be spoken aloud.

"No," he said and using both his hands, he pushed her thighs open and lowered his face to her, running his tongue over her and slipping it inside of her. She arched her back and soft sighs escaped her. He was slow and gentle at first, kissing her body with his lips and his tongue, giving her intense pleasure and bringing her to orgasm over and over, but as she came for him each time, he grew more and more hungry for her and after a while he raised himself up and trailed his tongue along her belly to her breasts, and he began to rub his erection against the outside of her.

She closed her hands around the back of his head and moaned as he ran his tongue slowly and deliberately over the width of her nipples, wetting them and rubbing his lips over them, and then flicking them with the tip of his tongue. She wrapped her legs around him in growing need, but he continued to move the length of himself against the outside of her, sliding against her moist body and building the heat between them.

Reed's hands and fingers occupied her breasts then, and he brought his hot mouth to hers, licking her lips and sucking on her tongue, kissing her deeply and teasing her mercilessly. He closed his eyes and moved his tongue over hers, twisting and turning it, moving his mouth as though she was his to own and control and in his mind, somehow the kiss faded to the night before and the lips he tasted suddenly belonged to Jillian, and the body he hungered for beneath his was no longer Daisy's, but Jillian's.

White hot need rushed through him and he could not hold himself back. He angled his erection and plunged it into her, driving it as far as he could and she gasped and cried out in pleasure as he began to move in her, his hands clasping her body, gripping her curves desperately as though he wanted to hold all of her at the same time, and he pushed himself into her depths over and over again, his breath becoming loud moans of pleasure and desire.

Daisy clasped her legs tightly around him, and held her hands on his back as he rocked himself into her as he had never done, and all the while, all Reed could see was Jillian in his mind. The blue dress was gone and she was lying underneath him, wanting him, needing him, crying out in bliss from his lovemaking as he delved his solid erection deeply into her and kissed her until she was breathless. He imagined the big breasts in his hands were hers, that the nipples in his mouth were dark and hard and that her long silky black hair was splayed out beneath them, and he pressed himself as far into her body as he could, heat and raging passion growing in him as he kept his eyes closed and kissed the lips that he imagined were hers, sucking and biting them gently as she orgasmed for him time and again and finally he could no longer hold himself back.

He shoved himself as far as he could into her hot body and came in an explosion of overwhelming pleasure. It stiffened him from head to toe, it stole his breath away, and then it weakened him to the point that he collapsed on top of her and thought the world might well have ended.

"Oh my god, baby. That was amazing. It's never been like that. Ever. I can't even count how many times we've screwed and you've never been like that with me." Daisy covered his forehead and his cheeks in kisses. "God that was incredible!" she gushed happily and held him close.

Reality came rushing back in and he opened his eyes and looked up at Daisy. "Well," he said quietly, "I do what I can."

She kissed his mouth full and hard, and then he lowered his head and rested it on her breasts. He couldn't believe he had imagined Jillian. He was screwing Daisy, and she was easily one of the hottest women he knew. How could he imagine another woman in her place? How could he imagine a woman that hated him? It was astounding to him for a few long moments but then he reasoned that he was because he was so angry with her and he knew that she was going to cost him his entire life, and this was nothing more than a way of mentally gaining control over her.

That's all it was. A method of control. Making the one girl who didn't want him at all suddenly need him and desire him so much that she was completely under his control and he was screwing her; making her come, making her kiss him and ache for him. That had to be about control.

He thought about it too much and before he knew it he was hard as a rock again. Daisy giggled and reached her hand down to rub his erection. "Do you want to do that again, baby? I'm all for it," she said with a grin. No, he thought. He didn't want to do that again. He couldn't stand the idea of coming that hard again because he was imagining that woman.

"No. Come down here and take care of me, Daisy. Make me feel better," he said lazily.

She shrugged and moved down the bed, straddling his legs and leaning over him until her face was beside his groin. "You know, I can't believe you finally came inside me. You never do that," she said without a care, but with no small amount of surprise.

He hadn't thought about it, but as she said it, he realized she was right. It was a cardinal rule of his never to ejaculate inside a woman. Any woman. It was how he helped to insure that there would be no children, and though he knew it wasn't a foolproof plan, he followed it religiously. His eyes flew wide open and he picked his head up and stared at her in horror. She smiled at him. "Don't worry, baby." She kissed the tip of his erection gently. "I'm on birth control. We're safe."

 He gazed at her for a moment and then propped the pillows up behind his head so he could watch her as she licked and sucked him, rubbed her fingers over him and aroused him to the point that he twisted his fingers into her blonde curls and began to pump himself into her mouth in a frenzy until he came again, and then he passed out from a mixture of exhaustion, sadness and booze.

Jillian stayed in her bed as long as she could the next morning, but she knew she would have to get up and face her mother at some point, so she finally did. She dressed nicely and walked out to the kitchen. Her mother was sipping tea and reading the newspaper.

"Good morning, Mother," she said quietly, pulling her hair up into a loose bun.

"It is a good morning," Kimiko responded. "How was your date last night?" she asked without hesitation.

Jillian was ready for her. "We went to dinner, then he drove me up into the hills to see the sunset, and then he brought me home."

Her mother looked at her intensely. "How was the date?" she repeated.

Jillian shrugged and focused on the teapot in front of her. She didn't want her mother to see her eyes, puffy from tears the night before. "The restaurant was really nice and the food was good. The sunset was lovely."

Kimiko set her tea cup down and smacked the newspaper down on the table. "Come here."

Jillian sighed and turned toward her mother, walking over to the table and sitting across from her. "Yes, Mother?"

"Did you show Reed a nice time? Was he happy with you? Will there be another date?" she leaned forward and pierced her daughter with her gaze.

"Reed liked me quite a bit. I don't know if there will be another date."

"He didn't ask you for another date before he left?" Kimiko pushed.

"No," Jillian said shortly.

Kimiko snorted and sat back in her chair. "Well, there's more to discuss," she said and sipped her tea again.

Jillian looked up at her. "What?"

"Your father is on his way to your uncles in Japan. I've talked with them and discussed this situation of yours with them and it has been decided that you will marry Reed if he asks you to be his wife."

Jillian dropped her tea cup and it hit the table but didn't break. "*What?*" she asked in shock.

"You will marry him if he asks you to. It has all been arranged," her mother answered her.

"Mother, no! I can't marry him! I just met him and I don't know him at all! He's atrocious and has absolutely no respect and no manners! I can't!" Panic and anger flashed up inside Jillian and her heart leaped into her throat.

Her mother looked at her calmly. "It has been decided. You will marry him. This is not an option for you; you have no choice in the matter."

Jillian felt like her whole world was turning inside out. She was going to be made to leave her home and her family and marry a man she never wanted to see again. It was the worst possible turn of events in her life. Her mind went to Wilson and her heart ached for the man she had wanted to marry, the man who had lied to her and told her he loved her, and then gone behind her back to marry someone else. Now she was being forced to marry a man who could not have less respect for her. Her life would be a never ending nightmare.

"Mother, no! I can't! Please don't make me go through this, please reconsider and listen to me! I don't want him!" she begged and pleaded.

"Jillian, you will marry him if he asks you to," Kimiko said sternly and resolutely.

"But I don't love him! How can you even think of making me marry a man I don't love? Please, Mother!" Tears ran in rivulets from her eyes down her cheeks, but her mother looked at her with a stony expression and raised her voice.

"The decision is made and the discussion is over! You may go!" Kimiko made it clear that she wanted her daughter to leave the room, and Jillian jumped up and ran first to her own room, but she paused at the door. She would find no solace in there and she knew it.

She needed her daddy. She ran to his dojo, knowing he wasn't there, but craving as much of his presence as she could find, and there was no place in their home where he was more present than in his dojo. She spent the day in there, weeping until she fell asleep and wrestled with nightmares.

Reed woke up the next day and discovered he had passed out in the pool house beside the swimming pool at his home. He couldn't remember getting there from the yacht. He looked over and saw that Daisy was curled up at his side, clinging to him. She must have driven him home. He peeled himself from her and covered her nude body with the sheet, then walked out of the sliding glass doors to the deck off the guest room in the pool house.

It had already been two days. He would have to get in touch with Jillian; she was his only chance. She hated him, and she never wanted to see him again, but he wasn't going to let the week run out without at least trying to change her mind.

He called her cell phone number and it rang a few times and then she answered it. He was incredulous. He hadn't expected her to do that. He thought perhaps she didn't know who it was.

"Hello," she said quietly. She knew.

"Hi, Jillian, this is Reed."

"Yes," she replied.

"I wanted to apologize for my behavior, I feel really bad about it. I had no business treating you that way, as you said, and I'm really sorry about it." It wasn't entirely a lie, he did regret it, but he wasn't sorry at all that he had gotten to kiss her and hold her. He pushed the thoughts from his mind and focused on the phone call.

"Okay," she said in a monotone voice.

"I was hoping I could talk with you today. Right away, actually. There's uh… there's something kind of imperative that I need to discuss with you. Ask you. Talk with you about…" he began to stammer. "Um, could you just please come over as soon as you are able to? I'm at my house." He felt like he was begging, and he didn't want to sound desperate, but he did want her to understand just how important this was to him.

"Fine. I'll be there when I can." She hung up the phone and buried her head in her pillow.

She knew that she was going to have to say yes to him if he asked her, and she knew there was no way out of it. She had cried so much in her father's dojo the day before that she was all cried out and she had resigned herself to her fate. She rose up from her bed and pulled a sundress on, then tied her hair up in a loose bun. There was no sense in putting off the inevitable. She picked up a pair of sandals and walked barefoot to the front door.

Kimiko emerged from her office and looked at her daughter with questioning eyes. "Where are you going?" she asked.

Jillian turned and looked directly at her mother, and with an unfeeling monotone, replied, "I'm going to see Reed."

Her mother handed her a set of keys. "Take my car. If he asks you, you say yes."
Jillian nodded, pulled her sandals on and walked out the door.

Reed hung up and placed his hands on the railing of the deck. How on earth was he going to ever get her to agree to marry him? He considered begging and pleading, he thought momentarily of trying to romance her, but she seemed impervious to his romantic talents. She was the only woman on the planet who seemed to be immune to his charm.

He sighed and looked down. Bare hands began to rub his back and shoulders, and then reached around from behind him to massage his chest. "What's the matter with my baby?" Daisy cooed at him, laying her head on his back. She slipped her hands into his shorts and began to rub his groin. "Want me to make you feel better?" she smiled and kissed his back.

"Not now, Daisy. I can't. I'm sorry," he said, pulling her hands from him and walking back into the pool house. He passed a mirror and realized that he hadn't showered in two days and he looked like it. If he was going to convince Jillian to marry him, he should at least look the part of the billionaire fiancé. He pulled off his shorts, stepped into the shower and lost himself in the steam.

It was the best he had felt since his orgasm into Daisy when he had imagined she was Jillian. He let the hot water run over his face and wished that it would wash the thoughts of her from his mind. He couldn't believe he had let himself imagine her as he had, naked, laid out beneath him, clinging to him, kissing him, crying out in pleasure for him.

He couldn't believe he had imagined himself inside of her, moving in her, feeling her hot body squeezing his erection, his mouth on her black breasts, his hands all over her body, feeling her curves, his tongue entwined with hers and then finally coming harder and deeper than he had ever orgasmed in his life, and inside of Daisy! What had he been thinking?

He realized he had been thinking about it too much again, because he was rock hard and desperate for release. He stepped from the shower and walked out into the pool house nude and dripping wet, stiff with desire. His bright blue eyes scanned the room. "Daisy!" he yelled. She came in right away, emerging from the bedroom and grinning when she saw him.

"Hey baby!" she said, walking up to him and wrapping her arms around his waist. "You look like you're ready for some fun. Do you want to go into the bedroom?" she asked with a grin.

"No," he said, almost gruffly. He grabbed her face in his hands and kissed her hard, moaning loudly with urgent need, and then he lifted his face from hers, leaving her breathless and he looked down at her. "I need you. I need you now." He reached beneath her chin and grabbed the edges of her robe, pulling it open and then he dropped it unceremoniously to the floor.

His hands closed firmly on her breasts and he bent and covered her nipples with his mouth, sucking at her with an insatiable hunger for her flesh. He told himself it would only be once more. He told himself that this would be the only other time he would do it.

He closed his eyes and the nipple in his mouth became dark and hard, her breast became black, as did the rest of her body, and in his mind, her hair turned from golden curls to a long straight glossy black curtain. He moaned again with desperate need and Daisy gasped beneath his mouth as it ravenously devoured her flesh. He leaned up and kissed her mouth again, hard and anxiously, needing… wishing…

"Turn around," he whispered hoarsely, grabbing her waist and turning her in his arms. He bent her over and touched her core, softly at first, and then as his need grew irrepressible, he slid his fingers in and out of her, drawing the heat and moisture in her out until his hand was soaked. He grasped her waist and thrust himself inside of her, imagining that the woman he was burying himself so deeply in was Jillian.

He had no idea why he wanted to imagine it so desperately, why she turned him on this way as no other woman ever had, why he needed to pretend that it was her, but the fantasy was like oxygen to him just then, and he felt as though he needed nothing more than that with her.

He held tightly to Daisy's hips and pushed himself into her over and over, crying out loudly with pleasure as he planted himself so deeply into her body, eyes closed, pretending. His orgasm was going to be strong, perhaps even stronger and harder than the first one. He could feel it culminating, the pleasure, her exotic beauty, he was intoxicated with the fantasy of being inside her, and then he heard something that turned him ice cold all the way to his soul.

"Reed!" she cried out.

He opened his eyes and saw Jillian standing before him in the doorway of the pool house, and everything in the universe came to a grinding halt. Her mouth was open in shock and horror as she took in the scene before her. Reed was standing nude behind a blonde woman, who was bent over as Reed had intercourse with her from behind her.

Jillian had started at the front door of the house and Reed's brother Anderson had opened the door to her, smiling and chuckling when he saw her. He introduced himself and told her that Reed was in the pool house waiting for her and she should head into the back garden and go see him.

She hadn't understood why that was humorous to him, but he had led her right to the pool and pointed to the door of the pool house, telling her to walk right in.

She hadn't expected to find what she was looking at now. She had thought she couldn't possibly be more disgusted by Reed, but she had been wrong. She turned her head away and closed her eyes, feeling as though she might vomit right there if she had to look on the scene even a moment longer.

"Reed!" she repeated, her stomach in her throat, "How could you!" she cried out, sickened.

He felt just as sickened as she was. He was horrified that she had caught him as she had. He mentally berated himself for his weaknesses and condemned his desires. If he lost his inheritance, his home, his family, his whole life because he was screwing Daisy while imagining it was the woman he was supposed to marry, he would never forgive himself.

Everyone seemed frozen for a moment, but then Jillian turned and walked out of the door, slamming it behind her and Reed pulled himself from Daisy who was silent with shock and curiosity as to who the woman was who had just left them. Reed reached to the floor and grabbed Daisy's robe, pulled it on over his body and ran as fast as he could out the door after Jillian.

Anderson waved to him from the back door of the house and then smiled and walked back inside. Reed growled under his breath and saw Jillian a short way ahead of him; she was running through the garden. He chased after her, calling her name loudly, and finally, she stopped and a minute later, he caught up with her.

She kept her back to him, but he walked up close behind her. "Jillian, I am so sorry. You have no idea how sorry I am. That was a mistake, and that woman means nothing to me, truly. Listen, you can't be upset about that, I know you were seeing that guy Wilson and you wanted to be with him. Don't act like your heart is hurt or anything."

She gasped at the sound of Wilson's name and he knew he had hit a soft spot with her.

He reached his hand out and gently laid his fingertips on her shoulder. "Please, Jillian, please turn around. We have to talk," he pleaded softly and waited for her.
She knew she had no choice. She turned slowly and looked at his chest, not wanting to look into his eyes.

He dropped his hand from her and stood before her, mostly covered in Daisy's thick white pool robe. "Listen, I'm so sorry that you just walked in on that. That wasn't supposed to happen, not ever. It just... kind of..." he stammered.

She closed her eyes trying to erase the image of him with the blonde from her mind. "You disgust me," she said quietly.

He stared at her. "I don't doubt it," he said softly. "Quite frankly, I disgust myself, most of the time, but nobody cares enough for me to change it, least of all me."

She looked up at him and narrowed her eyes. He looked absolutely beautiful standing there in the white robe with his black hair tousled and wet, hanging down and framing his bright blue anxious eyes.

"What do you want to talk with me about? Why am I here?" she asked, wishing she could get it over with quickly and be gone.

"I have to talk with you… to… ask you… I… um…" he stopped short and looked around them. "We're in the atrium…" he said in disbelief. He pointed to one of the stones in the path; the corner of it was raised slightly higher than the rest of the path. "I tripped on that stone and lost your bracelet here. I'm so sorry about that, too, Jillian.

"Listen, um… I… god, I feel like all I've done is apologize to you over and over for all the mistakes I keep making." He ran his hand through his wet hair and looked away from her, a strange look of something like desperation came over his eyes and he looked back at her.

"Jillian, look, I know you have no reason to like me, or even to talk to me. You said you never wanted to see me again, and I believe you. I'm not sure I ever want to see myself again…" he almost laughed, but he wasn't really joking. "This might seem way out in left field, but… uh…." He stopped and looked at her and then lowered himself awkwardly to one knee and looked up at her.

She knew it was coming then. She didn't know how on earth it was even happening, but it was coming straight for her like a freight train. She closed her eyes and looked away, swallowing her grief and despair.

"Will you marry me, please?" he asked, his whole life was resting in her hands and he felt ridiculous, but he had to take the chance because he couldn't risk the possibility that she might say…

"Yes," she said in a low, tired voice.

Everything in him stopped. He blinked. "What?" he asked, looking up at her. Her head was turned away from him and her eyes were closed. She couldn't have said what he thought he had heard her say. She turned her head slowly to him and opened her eyes.

"I said, yes," she repeated.

He felt relief wash over him like a maverick wave, and the sun shone on him again as though it was his birthday, Christmas, New Year, and he was the winner of the gold at the Olympics, all at once. He stood up slowly and stared at her as a smile grew wide over his face.

"Why?" he asked. He couldn't help himself.

"Because I have to," she said quietly. "My parents have given me no other choice."

He nodded solemnly. "That's fair," he replied.

She looked up at him and said, "Why did you ask me?"

He let a little smile cross his face. "Because my father gave me no other choice." He looked down at her and he tilted his head a little. "Thank you, Jillian, you've really saved me."

She shook her head and closed her eyes, biting her lip to keep from crying and then she said quietly, "Well, at least one of us got saved by it." Then she turned and began to walk away from him.

"Wait! Um… where are you going?" he asked, catching up to her.

"To tell my mother she has a wedding to plan," Jillian said in her monotone voice.

"Jillian…" he spoke gently to her and she looked up at him, caught up momentarily in his bright blue eyes. "You won't regret this. I promise. I won't make you regret this, not for a single day."

"I hope not," she said, and walked away.

Chapter 5

When Jillian told her mother that she and Reed had become engaged, Kimiko was beyond pleased, and immediately went into her office to phone her family in Japan and Jillian's father, Samson, as well as Reed's father, Carter. Carter and Kimiko began to discuss engagement parties and wedding plans and hinted at discussing business plans shortly after the wedding.

Jillian and Reed saw each other in the company of their parents several times over the course of two weeks, and each time she was quiet and withdrawn, having almost nothing but greetings to say to him. Each time Reed saw her, he grew increasingly fascinated by her and equally nervous about what they were committing to. He stole moments when no one was watching him, staring at her body, her hair, her skin, wondering about her, and being simultaneously intrigued by her, and put off by the indifferent manner she had toward him. No woman he had ever met since puberty had been indifferent to him. Not one, until Jillian.

Carter was a billionaire with two sons; Reed, the oldest, a partying playboy of the first order and who had done nothing but bring shame and embarrassment to his family and their businesses, and Anderson, the younger son, who worked tirelessly to build the business up, bring in new deals, make money and go along behind Reed, cleaning up his messes and paying small fortunes to compensate for the damage Reed left in his wake.

Carter had demanded that Reed either marry Kimiko's daughter Jillian, or be disinherited and evicted from the family home and the family, because he had gone too far with his unadulterated, wild lifestyle. After much consternation and one date gone very wrong, he was told he had to propose to Jillian.

Jillian was under her mother's thumb, ruled by a traditional Japanese heritage, though she felt much more connected to her

African American father and identified much more with being black than Asian.

Their home was designed entirely around Japanese culture, as were their lifestyles. Her mother's three brothers, who lived in Japan and operated technology companies there that were the cornerstone of the tech industry, had mandated that Jillian marry Reed, as they considered it a perfect opportunity to expand throughout the United States through Carter's wealth and connections.

It was a business marriage right from the start, and while both Reed and Jillian had objected to it from the very beginning, Jillian more so, they both knew they had no real choice; Reed would be alone and broke, and Jillian was being forced by the sheer power of her mother and uncles. She had no alternative.

The news of their engagement brought a great deal of pleasure to their parents, but when Carter told his younger son, Anderson, Anderson was not happy at all to hear about it. Anderson was quite certain that Reed would fail at an epic level and be pushed out of their lives, and then he would never have to clean up his brother's public scandal messes again, and he would inherit the family money, businesses, houses, cars, the yacht, and the rest of it.

He would be the one in control, and would finally have all the benefit for the work he had done over the years. The news of their engagement meant that Reed would be inheriting everything, and Anderson would be his second.

Anderson entered Reed's room an hour after Carter had told him the news.

"Reed! You old dog. Get up! I've got a surprise for you," Anderson said with a wry smile.

Reed opened his eyes as his brother pressed the window shade button and the blinds opened, letting in brilliant shafts of sunlight. He closed his eyes and groaned.

"Hung over, brother? It's noon. It's time you got out of bed. Besides, you'll want to get up when you hear what I've got to tell you." Anderson walked into Reed's closet and kept talking, though the sound was muffled.

"Dad told me that you and Jillian got engaged. I didn't think you would be able to go through with it. Especially after she caught you red handed with Daisy. You really do amaze me sometimes, Reed. The only woman in the world who doesn't want you and you still get her to say yes to a marriage proposal minutes after she caught you screwing a stripper.

"It boggles the mind. Not that I blame you for screwing that stripper, mind you, Daisy is one hot little number. I wouldn't mind screwing her myself, truth be told, but I would have bet the inheritance that you wouldn't have gotten Jillian to marry you, and now, look at you. I guess it's a good thing I'm not always a betting man."

He walked out of the closet with a packed bag. "I'm going to bet, though, that you have a real good time for the next few days, because brother, I am sending you off to Vegas. Congratulations on your engagement. Now, don't worry about feeling lonely, I've made sure you'll have some company along the way. Daisy is going to go with you."

Reed climbed out of bed, fully nude, and walked to his bathroom. Anderson turned his head away from his brother. In the grand genetic scheme of things, Anderson got good business sense; he had brains enough for two people, but Reed got all the good looks. Reed had the chiseled body of a Greek god, as well as stunning looks, with his black tousled hair, bright blue eyes and winning smile. Anderson disliked being reminded of it and seeing his brother walk across a room nude was as blatant a reminder as there could be. Anderson waited for Reed to come back in to him, and he noticed with gratitude that Reed was getting dressed.

"I can't go to Vegas, I have to meet with Jillian's parents," he said morosely.

Anderson smiled at his brother and patted him on the shoulder. "Don't you worry about that! I'll explain that you had to take a business trip for me. No problem. This is my gift to you, so you can't turn it down. Happy bachelor party, brother."

Reed looked right at him, a smile creeping over his face, his eyes lighting up. "Really? You'll take care of everything with Jillian for me and I can get the hell out of here?"

Anderson nodded. "Nothing would make me happier than taking care of the Jillian situation for you, brother. Now, your bag is packed, the private jet is waiting at the airport for you, and I'm having the car pick Daisy up on the way. Go have a good time."

Reed didn't have to be told twice. He hugged his brother, grabbed his bag and was on the way to Daisy's within fifteen minutes. Anderson went back to his office. He had a lot of work to do.

Daisy climbed into the car in a short shiny little skintight dress and high heels. She squealed when she saw Reed.

"I'm so excited to see you and go on this trip! I couldn't believe it when your brother called me. I didn't even know he had my number, but he called and asked if I wanted to go on a little trip with you to Vegas!

"My boss is super pissed at me, but I don't care. I told him my mom was sick and I had to go help her, and he believed me. I think. I'm just so excited to see you!" She crawled onto his lap, facing him, and proceeded to kiss him sensually as she ran her hands over his chest.

"We're going to have such a good time, baby. Thank you." She hugged his neck and then sat beside him and he looked at her with a grin and popped open a bottle of champagne.

"Here's one for you…" he said, handing her the bottle. Then he poured himself a full glass of scotch. "…and one for me."

He toasted her and they started drinking and kissing, making out a little bit, and talking about what they wanted to do on their trip.

By the time they got to the plane, Daisy had polished off her second bottle of champagne and she headed straight for the bedroom at the back of the plane. She and Reed started to make out and she got as far as pulling his shirt off him before she passed out on the bed and he was laying there beside her with his pants still on, looking disappointed and bored.

He stood up and walked out of the bedroom, closing the door behind him and lowering himself into one of the recliner seats in the cabin. Almost immediately, their flight attendant appeared at his side with a wide smile on her face.

"Hi, Reed." She grinned at him. "I'm so glad to see you; it's been forever since you were on a flight. Usually it's your father and brother who take the plane. Can I get you anything?"

He looked up at her and smiled back. "Hey Gina, you look as lovely as ever." He winked at her. "Yeah, would you bring me a bottle of scotch, please?"

She disappeared and was back in no time with a full bottle of scotch. She opened it for him and he took a long pull off it and then looked up at her. She reached her hand over and slipped her fingers through his tousled dark hair and said softly, "Is there anything else I can do for you…" she trailed her fingertip down the side of his cheek and along his jaw, "…to make you more comfortable?"

His mouth curved up into a sly smile and he reached over to her leg and slid his hand up underneath her skirt, moving his fingertips up her thigh slowly. "What did you have in mind?" he asked.

"Oh Reed," she said softly, and bent over near his face, running her hand over his bare chest and pressing her lips to it softly, looking up at him with hungry blue eyes, "when it comes to you, I always have everything…" she kissed his chest again, slowly and softly, "…in mind."

"That's my girl, Gina." A smile was spreading over his face. He moved his hand up her thigh until he reached her panties. He slid them aside and began to rub his fingertips over her, massaging and stimulating her as she closed her eyes and gasped.

She stretched one leg over him, straddling his lap, and she unbuttoned her blouse and pulled it off, throwing it on the floor along with her bra. He grinned and while his hand was still bringing her enormous pleasure between her thighs, his other hand moved behind her back and pulled her toward him. She grew more excited as he licked and sucked at her small perky breasts and moved his fingers further inside her, manipulating her internally.

She lowered her face to meet his and leaned in to kiss him long and sensually, running her tongue slowly over his and sucking gently on the tip of it. Reed kissed her back, nibbling at her a bit, and then turned his attention to her pointed nipples, sucking hard at them, and she let a little moan escape her lips.

"It's been ages since you were here," she said longingly. His fingers danced inside of her nimbly and in no time, she was crying out softly as orgasm after orgasm stole away her breath and she clung to his head, holding it to her breasts. Finally, she sighed happily and kissed his lips softly and seductively again, and then Gina lowered her mouth to his chest and one slow, wet, lingering kiss at a time, she made her way down his chest to his waist. Then she opened his pants and slid them down a bit. She gasped and giggled. "I love it that you almost never wear anything under your pants."

Her kisses moved to his thighs and to where he was stiff with desire. She fondled him and kissed him, running her hot tongue slowly up and down his shaft, looking up at him as though she was playing with something that she had finally caught.

Her lips slid over the tip of him and he took a huge swig of his bottle just as she began to suck on him. Reed closed his eyes and reveled in the absolute pleasure he was feeling. He had done just about everything with Gina at one point or another, every time he was on the plane, but her favorite, and his when he was with her, was what she was doing with him just then.

He pulled the pins from the bun in Gina's hair and her wavy brown hair fell over his thighs. He loved the tickle of it. She began to suck on his erection more intensely and he pushed his hips forward toward her, groaning happily and sliding his hands through her hair to the back of her head, pulling her face closer to his groin and pushing himself further into her hot, wet mouth.

Gina had a way of making him feel extraordinarily good without bringing him too close to an orgasm, and it lasted a long while, every time she did it. Her sucking and licking seemed more determined this time, more intense, and finally he could not hold himself back and he grasped the back of her head tightly as he climaxed, buried in her mouth, as the full force of his ejaculation escaped him, and then he sagged back into the depths of his chair.

She played a little, kissing him softly and then looked up at him from his lap.

"Gina…" Reed said softly as he played with her hair. "Do you do this for anyone else in my family?" he asked curiously.

She shook her head and kissed his thigh, then looked back up at him. "No. Your father would never do something like this with me, and Anderson has tried a couple of times but I always tell him no. He knows I do things with you and I think he's been jealous for a long time, sort of thinking that I would take care of him as well, but I'm just not interested in him. I'm way too taken with you." She grinned and ran her hand over his chest.

"Well, I'm flattered." He smiled down at her. "You are one lovely looking lady." He winked at her again and took another huge swig of scotch.

They landed in Vegas and Reed had to wake Daisy up and help her off the plane. Their limo took them to the Venetian and they checked into their suite. Anderson had gone all out. The bar was overstocked, the mini kitchen was filled with food, there were tickets to several shows waiting for them on the desk, fresh fruit and chocolate in various places around the place, and no end of champagne and roses everywhere. It looked more like a honeymoon suite.

Daisy squealed and ran to the bed and jumped on it. She had gotten her second wind and was ready to play with wild abandon in Las Vegas. Reed looked at her and laughed as she bounced up and down, and he walked over and planted his hands on her hips, pulling her to him and wrapping his arms around her.

She grinned at him and lowered her face to his, kissing him deeply and running her tongue over his, as his hands moved from her waist down over her hips to the very short hem of her shiny gold lame dress. His mouth and hers were both wet and hungry, but he shoved the bottom of her dress up over her hips, clamped his hands on her ass and buried his face in her crotch, focusing his hunger for her there. She gasped and moaned as he rubbed his tongue over the outside of her and then flicked the tip of it back and forth just inside her.

Reed groaned with desire, feeling his body stiffen, and he stopped tasting her long enough to pull her dress up over her head and throw it to the floor. His hands gripped her hips and he moved his tongue over her again, making her cry out with pleasure and clench her fingers in his wavy black hair. He moved his mouth up over her belly, kissing her and sucking on her skin, and his hands and mouth moved upward to her breasts, kneading them and pulling them to his ravenous mouth.

He sucked and bit at her nipples, pulling on them and running the width of his tongue over them and she leaned her face down to his, kissing his forehead and his cheeks until he lifted his face from her breasts and took over her mouth, kissing her with famished abandon.

He was fully aroused and he wanted to want her -- Daisy with her big fake breasts, her golden triangle of hair over the hot, wet core he loved to be in, her soft pink lips, her wild blonde curls, her sweet little ass, her pretty face and cute giggle… he wanted to want her, because he was scared that the last two times he had screwed her, he had closed his eyes and imagined she was Jillian.

He had never been more turned on than when he had been inside Daisy, imagining he was making love to exotic, stunning, beautiful Jillian.

Imagining his mouth was on her breasts, that the lips he was kissing were her dark lips, that the body he was clinging to was her curvy, delicious, petite body, that the skin in his mouth was her dark skin and the sounds of pleasure that emanated from his stripper girlfriend were instead coming from his incredible fiancé; a woman who wanted nothing to do with him and who had told him to his face that he disgusted her.

He didn't want to want her. He did not want to imagine her. He absolutely hated himself for closing his eyes and pretending he was with Jillian while he was with such a hot chick like Daisy, who completely adored him and let him do anything he wanted to her. He had decided that it was only about control; that it was about having the upper hand, since Jillian didn't want it and he was being forced to marry her.

He felt like his imaginations were a mental escape for him, to make believe that the only woman in the world who didn't want him was underneath him as he was moving deeply inside her, crying out in pleasure for him and what he was doing to her. He was sure that had to be it. Some form or method of acceptance and control.

He'd done it twice, though, and the second time, Jillian had caught him in the act because Anderson had sent her to the pool house to find Reed. Anderson knew Reed was in the pool house with Daisy. Anderson sent Jillian in anyway, and she had caught him mid-coitus as he was imagining he was inside of her. It was the worst possible scenario, he thought. He didn't want her to invade his senses like that, to make him want her so much that he closed his eyes and imagined her instead of the sexy little blonde who was constantly interested in pleasing him.

It was important to him that he keep his eyes open this time, every time; that he was used to because he was with Daisy and she could easily have been a centerfold model. Daisy worshipped him and he was her first priority and what she loved most was screwing him.

He wanted desperately to focus on that and not on the mysterious and alluring woman who had agreed to marry him. He wanted to block her from his mind entirely and not wish that he was lusting after her. Reed had made up his mind that this trip was going to be all about the gorgeous little blonde who was setting him on fire just then.

He pushed her back on the bed and she fell into the pillows laughing. She spread her legs for him and looked down between her breasts at him. "What do you want, baby?" She always asked him that, what did he want. Anything he wanted. He was so lucky to have such a smoking hot woman ready to please him anytime he wanted, any way he wanted. He wasn't going to let Jillian into his mind at all. He grinned at Daisy.

"I want to see how many times I can make you come," he said with a sultry smile. He buried his face between her legs and slid his tongue over the outside of her and into the deep recesses of her so passionately that she lost count of her orgasms.

He kept his eyes open and focused solely on her. When she couldn't take anymore, he knelt on the bed and pulled her up to him, straddling his body, and sliding her down onto his stone solid erection, thrusting every inch of it into her as far as he could. He pumped himself into the depths of her body over and over, as he buried his face in her breasts and sucked hungrily at her lips and tongue.

He kept his eyes open. He called out her name. He pushed Jillian out of his mind and he screwed Daisy like it was the very first time, but he could not orgasm himself. His body wouldn't seem to cooperate with him.. He had a full erection. He was where he most wanted to be, and it couldn't have been any more erotic between the two of them just then, but no amount of her riding him like he was a stallion would bring him to orgasm. She laid him down on the bed and his erection disappeared down her throat; she sucked and licked, and kissed and teased, and he did not orgasm.

Reed growled to himself and rolled Daisy onto her back, laying between her legs and planting himself deeply inside her as she clung to him and he gorged himself on her hard pink nipples. Then he sighed in resignation and before he even had his eyes all the way closed, Jillian seeped into every part of his mind.

Her lovely smile, her beautiful dark eyes. The blue dress she was wearing on their first date. The feel of her body in his hands and her full lips as he kissed her. He imagined pulling the blue chiffon material off the full swell of her breasts and running his tongue over her dark breasts and nipples, the feel of her silky smooth black hair in his fingers, the softness of her rounded hips as he buried his arousal in her body.

He was rocked with desire and overwhelmed with passion as he moved within Daisy's body, his eyes closed, his mind and heart pretending is was Jillian. He groaned and cried out as he moved faster in her, his pleasure mounting furiously as he lost his breath and his whole body stiffened and he was torn between not wanting it at all and wanting it more than he had ever wanted that moment with any other woman.

He cried out, thrusting himself into the body beneath him, holding himself completely in her as his orgasm hit him full force and he exploded with bliss, every nerve ending in him tingling simultaneously. He shuddered and gasped as the last of the liquid left him and he lowered himself onto Daisy's breasts, his lungs heaving and his body exhausted.

"Oh my god, baby, that was amazing! You know," Daisy said, kissing his forehead, "that's the second time you've come in me. You never do that. Ever. It's so cool that you feel close enough to me now that you can do that. I think it means you're falling in love with me. Our sex life has never been as good as it has been the last few times.

79

"You're just unstoppable! I love it!" She tilted his face up to hers and stared dreamily into his bright blue eyes. "I love you, baby." She leaned down and kissed his lips and he groaned out of disappointment and agony.

She had shown him countless times how much she loved him, but she knew he didn't love her in return, so she had never said it. Since he had been imagining he was making love with his fiancé rather than screwing his hot stripper girlfriend, things had gotten very good in the sack between he and Daisy, but none of it had to do with Daisy.

He rolled off her and pushed himself up off the bed. Daisy watched him in utter happiness as he crossed the room and closed the bathroom door behind him, only to open it right back up and look at her.

"I shouldn't be coming in you. I don't want to get you pregnant. You did say you're on birth control, right?" he asked, furrowing his brow.

She smiled at him and nodded. "Sure I am. I'm a stripper. It would be stupid of me to not be on birth control."

He nodded with a look of uncertainty on his face and took a shower. He had a problem. He was seriously lusting after the one woman who wanted nothing at all to do with him.

Reed couldn't believe that Daisy couldn't make him come. It was just sex. She was easily one of the sexiest women he knew, and that was saying something. He couldn't figure out why he couldn't come until he closed his eyes and thought about Jillian.

He shook his head and made up his mind not to think of her again. He was in Vegas to have a good time with Daisy and that was what he was going to do.

They went down to the casino and gambled. They ate, saw shows, laughed and held hands and had a great time. They drank and he did everything he could think of to be turned on by the thought of Daisy.

He slid his fingers up under her tiny dress when they were in a crowd of people in the dark shadows on the sidewalk outside by the Bellagio fountains and no one saw him slip his fingers inside her and manipulate her until she came three times, biting her lip and holding back her gasps of pleasure.

He leaned her head into his chest as she came, hiding her face so she wouldn't give them away, and as she buried her face in his chest, he closed his eyes and Jillian was there in his mind, and it was then that he grew hard with need.

When he was in the shower with Daisy, washing her body and kissing her, he closed his eyes, and Jillian appeared under his lips and hands and he could not hold back the desire that engulfed him. He turned Daisy away from him and pushed his erection into her, eyes shut tight, hands reaching around to her breasts as he pretended he was inside Jillian, his hands on her body, and he came hard in Daisy.

He even tried keeping Jillian out of his mind when Daisy was sucking on his erections, but somehow he could not climax unless he closed his eyes, and he could not stand to think of Jillian's mouth on him that way, her beautiful sweet lips wrapped around him.

Each time he had pulled Daisy up onto his lap or laid her back in the bed, or turned her around away from him and in desperate need he had driven himself inside of her, and with each deep solid thrust into her body, he tried to push away the need for Jillian, but it only exacerbated his growing addiction.

The only way he could come was by closing his eyes and imagining that Jillian was the woman he was losing himself in and he hated it.

It was making him miserable and cranky and Daisy noticed fairly quickly. She asked him about it and he waved it off and said it was just family business that he was trying to keep his mind off of. It wasn't a lie, but he didn't want her to know what was going on. All she knew was that this was a spur of the moment trip that his brother had given him as a surprise.

When Reed realized that the only way he could orgasm was to think of Jillian, and when he finally admitted to himself that doing it was the most intense pleasure he had ever known, he succumbed to it, and became insatiably ravenous for the feeling, for the little pretend world where Jillian was his lover and she wanted him to please her, and where she wanted to please him.

He came in Daisy every single time he made love to her, and it quickly became making love, because what he wanted in his mind with Jillian was not just sex, it was not just screwing and having a fling, which was what he had always done with Daisy prior to his involvement with Jillian. The result of that was that Daisy believed Reed was in love with her and he just hadn't said it out loud yet.

She believed he was showing her by the way he constantly loved her and needed to be inside her like it was oxygen to him, and because he was coming inside her body every time rather than having her swallow it as he used to. He used to insist on it, but now it was the opposite. She began to tell him regularly that she loved him, and she glowed with the happiness of romance and love, and Reed grew darker inside, deeply bothered by what was happening.

***

Jillian was sitting in the Japanese garden of her home, feeding koi fish and enjoying the warm quiet moments in the sun. She knew her life would change soon and simple pleasures like this in her parent's garden would be long gone. She wasn't going to waste a single moment of them.

Kimiko came out into the garden. "Jillian, come here please." She spoke as though it was an order, not a request. She always spoke to Jillian that way. Her daughter rose up and walked to her, looking at her and waiting for her to continue.

82

"Yes, Mother?" she asked.

"Reed's brother Anderson wants you to come over to the house. He says he has some things to go over with you for the legal aspects of your marriage. He said since it's so late in the day that they would like you to stay for dinner and he asked that you pack an overnight bag so you can continue his discussions in the morning. Go as soon as you can." She turned and walked back into her office.

Jillian frowned for a moment. She wished earnestly she didn't have to go, but she shrugged her shoulders and packed a bag, then drove to Carter's gargantuan estate.
She pulled through the electric gate at the bottom of the drive and then wound her way up the hill until she got to the mansion. She was just stepping out of the car when a breeze caught her loose sundress and her hair, wrapping the white cotton dress snugly around her curves and pulling her hair free from the loose bun at the back of her head.

She heard a voice and looked up just in time to see Anderson coming toward her with a smile on his face. He took her hand and helped her from her car, closing the door after her and then he put his hands on her shoulders and drew her near to him, kissing each of her cheeks softly in turn, and then smiling down at her.

She tried not to look surprised when she looked up at him. He was very different looking than his brother. He had straight brown hair that was cut short and combed back. He had pale white skin and brown eyes. He smiled at her through thin lips and his smile didn't quite reach his eyes.

"How are you doing? My goodness look at you, you look really beautiful today. I'm lucky to have a woman as striking as you joining my family. My brother doesn't deserve you." He said it with deep meaning. The breeze picked up a little stronger and blew at her dress and her hair and she grasped the material, but her hair was tossed wildly for a moment and Anderson stood close in front of her

83

and reached up into her hair, pulling her hair pins out, allowing her hair to fall free.

It cascaded like a waterfall of black satin around her face, her shoulders and her breasts and Anderson stood before her, taking it all in. He lifted his hand and brushed it out of her face, slowly sliding his finger down the side of her cheek as he did so.

"You really are one of the most stunning women I have ever had the honor to know." He looked steadily into her eyes for a moment and then turned slightly to the side and offered her his elbow. "Shall we? Let's get you into the house and out of this wind."

She took his arm and he led her into the house and up the stairs to a guest bedroom on the second floor overlooking the pool and the pool house. She set her bag on the lounge at the foot of the bed and Anderson placed his hand on the small of her back, saying, "Come, look out the window. You can see so much from this room."

He guided her toward it, leaving his fingertips at the base of her back. "See, there are the gardens and over there is the atrium, which I understand you are already familiar with, there's the pool and oh... the pool house. I guess you've seen the pool house already. Perhaps I'll take you down for another look at it when no one is in it." He said quietly over her shoulder.

She gazed at the pool house remembering the last time she had seen it. Anderson had sent her out the back door to it looking for Reed. When she walked into the pool house she had found Reed having sex with a blonde woman and both of them were fully naked. She had hoped never to think of that memory again, but as Anderson mentioned it, it came back to her and she turned her head away in disgust.

Anderson slipped his finger beneath her chin and tilted her face up to him, looking into her eyes. "I'm sorry. How thoughtless of me to bring back such an awkward and uncomfortable memory for you. I don't know how he could look at another woman after seeing you. If it was me who was lucky enough to be marrying you, I don't think I would ever want to look away from you." His lips parted slightly and his thumb brushed over her chin. She blinked at him and he smiled and lowered his hand.

He walked over to her bag and tapped his fingers on it thoughtfully. "You know, Jillian, you're really making an enormous sacrifice for this marriage. You are giving up your entire life to marry my brother and spend the rest of your whole life with him." He spoke slowly and thoughtfully, looking down at her bag and then looking up at her. "It's really quite sobering to think of what you are doing at your family's behest; after all, you only just met Reed as an adult. Do you even have any feelings for him at all?" he asked, looking up at her.

She had been watching him until he asked her how she felt about Reed. "My answer is one that you probably wouldn't want to hear," she said quietly.

He nodded and smiled slightly. "It would be quite natural not to like him yet; you don't know him. Also, you've been exposed to him in a morally compromising situation and a shameful act. I wouldn't blame you at all if you were substantially less than impressed with him." He looked at her pointedly and tilted his head. "Are you?" he asked quietly.

She raised her head and looked directly at him. "I'm disgusted with him. I find him repulsive."

Anderson lifted his hand from her bag and walked back over to her, his eyes locked on hers as he drew close to her again. "I assure you, you have my every sympathy, but may I ask, why are you marrying him if you feel so badly about him?" Jillian saw that he was watching her closely and she felt like he was driving the conversation to some particular point.

"I am following my parent's request. Nothing more. It is my obligation," she replied quietly.

Anderson nodded understandingly. "My father was quite adamant that our family be connected to yours as well. He was anxious that

Reed should stop being such a wild playboy and settle down with a wife or else he would be evicted from the house and the business and lose his entire inheritance. My father is quite set on it. That's why Reed is marrying you." He stepped closer to her.

His voice softened and he gazed at her face, his eyes wandering from her eyes down over her cheeks to her full lips, where he paused for a moment, opening his lips ever so slightly, and then looked into her eyes again. "I wonder, though, if you know that there may be another option."

Jillian felt the tiniest surge of surprise and hope bubble up in her. "What would it be?"

Anderson smiled gently and raised his hand to her face, running his finger along the edge of her cheek and then holding it beneath her chin, lifting her chin up just enough so that her lips were nearer to his. He glanced at her mouth and then looked back into her eyes. "Well, perhaps I'm getting ahead of myself. Perhaps we should go see Reed before we really discuss other options or think about making any more *important* decisions."

Jillian's heart began to race and she wondered what other options Anderson was talking about. If there was a way for her to avoid marrying Reed, she wanted to know about it, but she felt as though Anderson might not be telling her everything, so she felt sure that the best thing to do just then was to wait and see what would happen before asking any further questions.

Anderson smiled at her and the tense air between them vanished. He walked over to her bag and picked it up, then held out his arm for her. "If we want to see Reed, we'd better be going. He's not at home just now, so we'll have a bit of a trek getting to him. Shall we?" he asked almost jovially.

She took a deep breath and slipped her hand in his arm again and he walked her outside where a limousine was waiting for them. She was seated in the car and as the driver pulled away, she looked back at the house, wondering what was going on and where Reed might be.

When the car pulled up near a private jet, she could not hold back her surprise. "What's going on? Where is Reed?" she asked, slightly concerned and hesitant.

Anderson, seeing her reticence, walked up to her and wrapped his arm around her shoulder, holding her close to him. "It's alright my dear, not to worry. Reed is in Las Vegas at the moment.

"We're just going to hop on the plane and nip down to see him. Really, it's nothing at all. I'm so very sorry if I worried you. Are you alright?" he asked, looking down into her face with careful concern.

Jillian looked up into his eyes and saw that things were fine and she felt he was being honest with her. "Yes, I'm sorry, I just wasn't expecting this."

He smiled sweetly at her. "No problem at all. Let's go." He lowered his hand from her shoulder to the small of her back and walked close beside her all the way to the plane. They boarded and she gasped at the luxurious appointments within it. Anderson smiled humbly.

"There's a bedroom in the back if you're tired and a full bathroom connected to it. This is the main cabin, and there is a full kitchen where our chef can cook up anything you'd like. Our flight attendant, Gina, can bring you anything you'd like." Gina nodded at Jillian with a wide smile.

They sat in the chairs of the main cabin and the plane took off. When it reached altitude, Anderson suggested a little tour. He walked her back to the bedroom and showed it to her, offering her a nap if she should want it, but she declined. She liked the bathroom on the plane; it had a shower and a tub. There was a small office area set up for two people. Gina was in the kitchen area, preparing sandwiches and pulled some fruit, meat and cheese trays from the refrigerator.

Anderson leaned onto the counter as he stood beside Jillian and looked pointedly at Gina. "Did you take especially good care of my brother while he was on his flight down to Vegas?" he asked with a hint of sarcasm. Gina blushed hotly and turned bright pink. Jillian noticed and felt her stomach tighten.

"I always take care of all of you," she said with a defensive tone as she shot Anderson a masked scowl.

He stood up and put his hands on Jillian's shoulders, holding her close to his chest from behind. "Well, not *all* of us," he said coldly, and then he turned and spoke to Jillian over her shoulder, his breath tickling her ear, "It's probably best to let Gina work. She will need to find some other way to earn her money on *this* flight."

He placed his hand at the small of Jillian's back and guided her back to her chair. Jillian hadn't missed Anderson's subtle references or Gina's furious blush. She wondered if she really wanted to know what they were talking about and thought better of it.

Anderson spent the rest of the flight asking Jillian about herself and he became increasingly fascinated with all of her answers. She felt like he understood her fairly well and like he might be someone in her new family who she could be friends with.

They landed in Vegas and a limousine took them to the hotel. Anderson had been texting on his phone and smiled widely as they were in the car on their way. He looked extremely happy.

"I've just sent Reed a message to tell him I have a little surprise for him," he confided in her, patting her thigh as she sat next to him in the car. Jillian smiled back at him a little, wondering how it was going to be to see Reed. She hoped it would go well, but she made herself swear not to have any expectations.

***

Reed opened the door of the hotel and the server wheeled in a candlelit service with champagne, chocolate, whipped cream and strawberries. "Compliments of your brother, sir," the man said, and then disappeared. Reed picked up his phone and saw that there was a text message from Anderson. 'I have a surprise for you.' Reed smiled and looked at the romantic spread before him.

88

Daisy bounded up beside him and giggled with glee. "Oh! Whipped cream... I could have some fun with that..." she grinned and dabbed a bit on her finger, popping her finger into her mouth and sliding it out slowly. Reed watched her and felt heat rising in him. She pulled his clothes off and dabbed some chocolate on her finger and then wiped her finger from his belly button downward. He watched her as she knelt before him and slowly licked the chocolate off him, and when the chocolate was gone, her tongue and mouth were occupied with his solid erection.

The harder she licked and sucked at him, the more he felt the urge to close his eyes and think of Jillian and the more aroused he became, until he could not stand it, and he picked Daisy up from the floor and walked her to the bed. She squealed with delight as he yanked her clothes off her and pushed her down onto the bed.

He was inside her in moments, his eyes closed, his hands grasping and groping her, his mouth hungrily tasting her dark skin, her dark nipples, his hands caught in her beautiful black satin veil of hair. His fantasies had gone further each time he had made love to Daisy, pretending she was Jillian, and this time it was the furthest he had ever gone.

He imagined her scent, the taste of her, her soulful dark eyes, the sound of her voice as he thrust himself deeply into Daisy over and over.

"Whisper my name..." he said, his mouth covering hers in a passionate kiss, "...tell me how much you want me. Tell me..." he sounded so desperate, even to himself. Daisy obliged immediately.

"Reed..." she whispered. "Reed, make love with me, kiss me, I need you, Reed, I want you so much. I love you, Reed."

He imagined the whisper was Jillian's, and it drove the passion in him to limits he had never conceived before. "Again!" he cried out as he grasped her breasts and buried his erection deeply in the hot depths of Daisy's body.

"Reed," came her whisper, "I need you, I want you inside me, touch me, Reed, touch my whole body, make love with me!"

His fantasy became real to him then. "Jillian! Ah, Jillian!" he cried out loudly as his orgasm exploded into Daisy's body, filling her as he ground himself deeply in her.

"*What!*" snapped Jillian, standing at the entrance to the bedroom, glaring at him with an open mouth and fury on her face.

"What?" asked Daisy, in confusion. She looked around and saw Anderson and another woman standing in the doorway to the bedroom. She gasped and grabbed Reed's shoulders, looking over his muscles at the intruders and Reed gasped and turned to see Jillian standing there, rage on her beautiful face; the face he had just imagined he was kissing. Anderson just stood behind Jillian, looking almost smug.

Reed jumped up from the bed and grabbed a sheet to cover himself from the waist down. Jillian didn't even bother to turn away from him this time; she just glared at him, piercing his eyes with hers. He looked positively horrified.

Anderson broke the thick moment of silence. "Well, brother, you've certainly done it this time."

"What are you doing here?" Reed breathed out heavily as he tried to catch his breath from his massive orgasm and his shock at Jillian's appearance.

"Who is she?" Daisy asked Reed, sitting up in bed and not bothering to cover her bare body.

"I might ask that same question," Jillian said, glancing at Daisy, "but this is the second time I've walked in on you, and I don't really care to know who she is."

"I brought her here," Anderson said to Reed, answering his question. "You may recall I texted you about it just a while ago."

Daisy stared at Jillian and her eyes widened. "It's you! From the pool house!" she cried out, pointing her sharp red fingernail at Jillian.

Reed gaped at his brother. "You said you had a surprise for me! I thought it was the strawberries and champagne you had delivered to the room!"

Anderson walked into the room, picked a robe up off the floor, and tossed it at Daisy. "Put something on, you're in decent company." He turned to look at his brother. "I ordered the champagne and strawberries for you and the lovely Jillian here to enjoy. I thought it might be a nice romantic gesture for you both." He walked back over to Jillian and wrapped his arm protectively around her shoulder.

She was filled with a rage that seemed to only grow more intense the longer she stood in the room.

Reed ran his hands through his hair in frustration. "I didn't know you meant you were bringing Jillian down here! This was supposed to be my bachelor party!" he shot at Anderson, trying to pin some of his shame and guilt on his brother, for bringing his fiancé to a hotel room he knew had his stripper girlfriend in it.

"Your bachelor party?!" Daisy repeated after Reed.

Jillian shook her head slowly. "You don't need a bachelor party, Reed, you aren't getting married." She turned around then and walked past Anderson, who bit his lower lip trying not to smile too widely. He didn't say anything at all. He just shook his head and followed Jillian out the door.

Reed watched them go and called out, "Wait! Jillian! Wait! Jillian, please!" but they were gone, and he was standing there, nude, beside a hotel bed with his lover staring up at him in angry revelation. He dropped the sheet from his hands and it hit the floor. There was no reason to cover anything up now.

Daisy jumped up off the bed and rushed to Reed. "Jillian? Is that the name you just called out while you were making love with me?" Tears rolled out of her eyes and down her cheeks and she smacked her hands on his chest. "Why did you call out her name? Who is she, Reed? Were you really going to marry her?"

He didn't say anything; he just looked at the floor, his whole world completely inside out. He was going to lose his family, his money, his family business, his inheritance, his past, his future, and all because he had lost Jillian.

The woman who had been plaguing his mind, who had been haunting his dreams and summoning up a white hot desire in him that he had never before known or felt.

Everything was gone, and for what? Because he had chosen to screw a stripper in a Vegas hotel room? He'd blown his whole life for sex with a stripper, and he wasn't even sleeping with her exactly, if he thought about it, every single time he had been intimate with her since the day on the yacht, he had imagined it was Jillian. He lost Jillian because he was addicted to pretending to make love to her.

"What about me!?" Daisy shouted at him as hot tears streamed down her face. She slapped her hands on his chest again and began to sob, falling against his chest and then pushing herself away from it again.

He snapped out of his train of thought and looked down at the naked woman standing before him, crying her heart out in agony because of him. It was the first time he had really looked at her as a person and not as his sexy little blonde lover. She was devastated.

"What about me?" she sobbed, slowly collapsing to the floor and crying uncontrollably. "I love you!" she wept bitterly.

In that moment, he realized what a monster he had been. In that moment, he saw the woman in pieces at his feet and it struck him like a hot iron that he had been using her since he had met her. He had used her body, her life, her emotions, her heart, and her future. He had used her all up like she was a disposable product that he could pluck up and drain the joy and pleasure from, and then toss back to the shadows when he had his fill. Then he would leave her waiting until he wanted her again. He sank to the floor beside her and placed his hands on her shoulders. "Daisy, Daisy, sweet, beautiful Daisy, I'm so sorry. I owe you the biggest apology on the planet. I have been unthinkably horrible to you. I've used you, I have never treated you with dignity and respect. I've never been serious about you or cared about you at all. I have only cared about myself, about what I wanted and desired, and I've never once put you first. I am so very sorry, my sweet friend."

She stopped sobbing and looked up at him through her wet eyelashes, blinking them and listening to him.

"Daisy, I never should have done all the things I've done to you, having you come to me at my beck and call, having you please me physically and then leave you alone. I've known all along how much you care about me, how you have tried to hide it from me so you wouldn't scare me away." He brushed her blonde curls away from her face.

"I love you," she whispered through her tear drenched sighs.

"I know. I know you think you do. The reality is that you can't really love someone who treats you the way that I have treated you. I need to let you go, Daisy, for your own good, so you can grow and be happy and live a life that has some meaning for you. Maybe find a nice guy and settle down; have a couple of kids or something." He wiped the tears from her cheeks and she reached up and grasped his hands with hers, her eyes widening in panic.

"No! You can't send me away! Is this about Jillian? Is this because you're getting…" she choked back a sob, "…married?"

He shook his head. "No, honey, this is so you can have a fresh clean start with no problems and no ties to your past, to me, to anything you've done. I'm going to give you some money to get you set up so you won't have to strip anymore, and you can just start again, make a new life without me in it, and you'll be so much better off."

She cried out as if she was in pain. "No! No… Reed, please don't do this!" She clung to him and pulled herself closer to him. "Please! You can't send me away, baby, I love you! I love you more than anything. I always have! I don't care if you're married, I won't mind, baby, you can just see me on the side, you can come play with me anytime you want to, and I will always be there for you!

"I won't tell anyone," she clutched his face in her hands and crawled up on her knees before him, "…it'll be our secret, and you can come and love me anytime you want to. I'll never tell anyone, I'll never let anyone find out, and then you can keep me! Please! Reed, please baby…" She kissed him and her wet tears soaked his face as she kissed his lips, his cheeks, his eyes and his forehead, pulling his face to her breasts and laying his head on her heart. "Please baby… don't send me away, let me love you no matter what… please!" She began sobbing again and he gently reached up and wrapped his hands around her wrists, pulling her hands from his face. He raised his head and looked directly at her.

"No, Daisy. You deserve so much better than me. You deserve someone who loves you back, and you might not be able to see that right now, but you will someday, one day when you are happy and in love with a great guy, you'll look back on this moment and thank me for letting you go." He stood up and pulled her to her feet.

She sobbed and pressed her face against his chest. "You can call me Jillian all you want to, baby, just please don't send me away, please… I'll pretend to be anyone you want, please…." She cried desperately and looked up at him, her arms wrapped around his chest.

He pulled her off of him and sat her on the bed. "No, Daisy. This has to be it. It has to be a clean cut so you can begin to heal right away. We can't draw it out, not even a little bit. Not even one time. This is it. We can't ever see each other or talk to each other again. I'm so sorry, sweet girl, I wish I hadn't done any of the things I've done to you. I wish I could take it all back. I don't want anything but the best for you, and I hope someday you find that."

Reed walked over to the desk and pulled a wad of cash out of his jacket hanging on the chair. He laid it on the desk. "Here, Daisy. This is enough money to get you going in a new life. I'm going to head out now, and I'll have a car ready to take you anywhere you want to go. Anywhere at all. Go ahead and shower and pack up your things. I'll have the car ready in two hours." He walked back over to her and pulled her up off the bed, sobbing miserably, and folded his arms around her, holding her gently to him and rocking her a little from side to side.

"It's going to be okay, honey, you'll see. It'll be so much better. Thank you, Daisy, for everything." He leaned down and kissed her cheek, he hesitated a moment and then he softly kissed her lips for a brief moment, and then he stepped away from her, pulled his clothes on, grabbed his jacket and walked out the door, leaving her wailing behind him.

He was positive he had never felt worse in his life. He went down to the bar and bought a bottle of scotch and then went to a private room and drank a good portion of it.

Jillian and Anderson walked out of the room and the door closed behind them. She didn't speak. She had no desire to say anything. Her mind was an explosion of chaos, anger, frustration, hurt and loss. Anderson stayed close to her and when the elevator doors closed, leaving them alone, he lifted his hand to her shoulder in comfort.

She closed her eyes and bit her lower lip, holding in all her pain and anger. She took a deep breath and let it out, hoping it would take all the negativity in her out of her and release it from her.

They walked out of the hotel and climbed into the limo. As they drove back to the airport, she looked out the window silently, trying

95

to sort things out in her mind. She had broken the engagement. She had called off the wedding and now she would have to answer to her mother. There was no way she could marry a man like Reed. How could she live with a man like that; share her life with him and have absolutely no chance at love.

Not that she expected it, far from it, but somewhere in the recesses of her heart, over the weeks since they had become engaged, she let herself believe somehow that it might be possible someday to develop some caring feelings for each other.

Anderson said nothing to her, he only stayed beside her, his hand at the small of her back, guiding her and reassuring her as they got onto the plane and he told Gina to bring a drink for them both. They took off and when they were at altitude, he walked over to her chair and held out his hand.

"Come with me, please. Let's go talk."

She looked up at him and sighed, taking his hand and standing up. He walked her back to the bedroom and closed the door behind them, handing her the drink that Gina had made for her. She shook her head at first for a moment, but then as she looked at it, she closed her eyes and shook her head and then took it from his hand and tilted it back, swallowing most of it fairly quickly.

Anderson smiled as she tilted it back again and emptied it. He handed her his glass. "Here. One more for the road," he said softly.

She took a little more time with the second one, but it too was gone in a few gulps. When her second glass was empty, she hiccupped and he laughed at her and took her hand in his, leading her to the bed and sat her down at the edge of it, then he sat beside her.

"I know you must be holding in a great deal of emotion, Jillian. I'm here for you. You can trust me. You can lean on me. Let me comfort you. I feel totally responsible for the situation. I should never have taken you to see him." He reached up and rubbed her shoulder, reaching his hand slowly toward her neck and her back, massaging her gently.

She shook her head, but then as he rubbed his hand over her back, she closed her eyes and let the walls fall down. She hadn't cried around anyone but her father and for the first time, she couldn't hold the pain in because she knew he wouldn't be home to hold her. He was still in Japan, and it was apparent that he would be staying there a little longer. She had no one to go to, no one to trust, to hold her and comfort her, and here was someone she barely knew but whom she felt she could trust and confide in.

Tears streamed down her cheeks and Anderson pulled her close to him, holding her snugly in his arms and wiping away her tears. "It's okay, Jillian, let it go, let it all go. Come here," he whispered to her as he pressed her face to his chest and rubbed her back.

"What am I going to do? I trusted him! I thought he was going to marry me and mean it! I thought he was going to be a real husband to me. I'm such a naïve fool," she wept and he rocked her a little as she cried on his shirt, wetting it with her tears. "I called off the wedding! My mother is going to kill me. She isn't giving me a choice, I don't have a choice in this!" She wept more and he leaned down to her ear, his lips close to her cheek.

"Yes, Jillian, you do have a choice," he whispered.

She couldn't stop the tears. "What choice? To marry a man who is constantly out sleeping with other women? What kind of a marriage is that?" Her tears fell heavy on his chest.

"Jillian," he whispered, placing his finger under her chin and lifting her face close to his, "You do have another choice, another option."

She looked at him in confusion, her dark eyes gazing up at him through her wet eyelashes and she remembered what he had said in the bedroom at the house earlier, something about another option.

She sat up and tilted her head, looking at him curiously. She sniffled and he reached up and gently brushed the tears from her wet cheeks. She blinked and reached up to get the last of her tears and he looked down at his shirt and smiled. "Would you look at me, I'm soaked."

"Oh no!" she whispered, "I'm so sorry!"

He only smiled at her and shook his head. "Don't worry about it, Jillian. You haven't done anything wrong at all, no need to apologize." He stood up and began unbuttoning his shirt slowly, his eyes on hers. "I'm so glad to do anything I can to help you."

When she realized he was taking his shirt off, she looked away and he chuckled at her. "Now, Jillian, you can't possibly be shy about seeing me without my shirt on," he said softly. "Not after you've seen my brother like you have."

She closed her eyes to hold in tears that threatened to spill again and Anderson put his finger under her chin, lifting it gently as he stood before her. She opened her eyes and looked up past his stocky muscular chest and arms to his eyes. He smiled at her.

"That's my girl," he whispered softly and sat close to her on the bed, reaching his hand up and brushing a stray tear from her eyelashes. He traced his fingers over her cheek and leaned closer to her. "Now, would you like me to explain about your other option?" he asked silkily.

Jillian nodded. Her head was growing very light. She shouldn't have had anything to drink, let alone two drinks, especially one right after the other. His hand felt warm on her cheek and it distracted her a little. "Yes, please," she whispered.

"Your parents are insisting that you marry Reed because they want to be in business with my family. Right?" he spoke gently, stroking her cheek with a feather soft touch.

She nodded. "Yes."

He shook his head. "My brother doesn't deserve a girl like you, Jillian. Someone so kind, so sweet and tender." He reached his hand up to the back of her head and pulled the pin from her hair and the long black satin curtain fell all around her shoulders. "So... beautiful..." he said, running his fingers down the length of her hair, looking at it shine in his hands and then raising his eyes to meet hers again. "I wonder if you realize what a profound effect you have on... people," he said, reaching to stroke her hair again, petting her gently.

Jillian felt comforted, but there was something else... something, she couldn't quite put her finger on. Some feeling she was completely unfamiliar with.

"You see, the truth is that Reed has been having an affair with the stripper you saw for a long time, and he's not going to give that up, not for you, not for anyone. He wouldn't give up any of his girlfriends, not even for marriage." Anderson slipped his hand behind Jillian's neck and began to massage her shoulder. She felt the stress there start to slip away, and a light dizziness begin to swim through her head.

"That's why our father told him to marry you; it was either that or be disinherited. He was going to lose everything, and his only chance to keep it was by marrying you. You don't know though, what the plan was if Reed didn't marry you, do you?" His voice had become quite soft and he was near enough to her that she could feel his breath on her skin.

"If Reed didn't marry you, I was going to have to assume his responsibilities and manage the business, which I have already been doing for years." His hand moved from the back of her neck to the side of her face.

"Now you have made a choice, you have decided that you can't live a life with Reed, that he isn't good enough for you, and you're right, Jillian," he stroked his thumb over her chin and she felt its warmth, "but you don't have to anger your parents and break your vow to them. You can still keep your word, help your family and connect our two families, by marrying me."

Her eyes grew wide in surprise and he smiled at her. "I know, it's a shock… it's a truly far fetched idea, but think about it carefully, Jillian. You'll be accomplishing the same promise you made to your parents," he was whispering, so close to her face, "you'll be fulfilling their wishes, and you will bring the families and businesses together, but you won't be trapped in a loveless marriage with a man who has an insatiable hunger for other women. You won't be locked into knowing that you would never be enough for Reed, and that he would always seek love in the arms of other women."

He continued to stroke her chin and the shock of the idea seemed to wear off as his words came slowly into focus.

"You would be with a man who admires you, who knows how special you are inside, who knows you and wants you, beautiful Jillian. You'll have a husband who will give you everything you want. Just… choose me, Jillian."

He leaned his mouth close to hers and the heat from him made her close her eyes to try to keep her focus even a little.

"Marry me, choose me…" he whispered, his lips barely touching hers as he spoke. She gasped slightly at the feel of them, and she had no time to think or react as his hand on her cheek held her to him and he closed his mouth over hers in a soft kiss, his lips pressing lightly against hers, feeling her, learning the curve of her mouth.

His lips parted and he touched his tongue to her lips as delicately as warm sunlight, barely grazing it, tracing the lines and swells, and then tentatively tasting her tongue, and pulling her close to him, holding her against his bare chest.

Jillian felt the dizziness swirling all throughout her and strange feelings flowing in her body. His arms held her so close to him that she could feel the heat of his body on hers and it made her heart pound.

He moved his hand from her cheek and combed his fingers through her long black hair. "You deserve to be wanted," he whispered, kissing her slowly, moving his lips over hers, "...I want you, Jillian."

She did want to be wanted, and Reed had made it clear that he wanted other women.

"You deserve to be loved all of your life..." He trailed his lips over her cheek to her neck and electricity followed his tongue and his lips as they canvassed her dark skin. He kissed her just below her ear. "I can give you that, Jillian," he whispered, moving his lips over her skin like he was breathing her in. "I can give you everything."

Her head was swimming and her body was warmer than she could ever remember it being. She reached her hands up his chest and held on to his shoulders, trying to stop the lightness in her head by anchoring herself to him.

"Have you made love with Reed?" he asked quietly.

"No," she whispered. Her answer made him smile.

He laid her back on the bed and she shook her head a little. "I'm not tired..." she tried to say, but his mouth closed over hers and he kissed her deeply, drawing up a fire in her belly she had never felt, and making her moan softly.

"That's it... let it happen..." he whispered, his lips kissing hers gently, opening her mouth with his. "That's my girl. Can you feel it?" He kissed her again, so very slowly, lingering on her lips and running his tongue over hers. "That's what you need. That's what you want, isn't it? This is what I want. I want you, Jillian. So much. Let me give you what you need, everything you need, all of your life, starting right now."

She forgot about the pain and anger that had seemed to saturate her whole being at the hotel and found herself getting lost in feelings

Anderson was bringing up in her. He might be right, she reasoned. He might be an option, she thought as his words echoed through her mind and his mouth moved softly over hers.

If she married him, she would still be bringing their families together. Did it really matter which brother she was with? She began to wonder if he wasn't right about it after all.

Anderson moved his lips to her cheek and kissed her lightly as his fingers traced trails over her neck. "Would you like a lifetime of this?" His mouth closed on her neck, kissing and sucking gently and she drew her breath in quickly and closed her hand over his arm.

"I…" she couldn't seem to catch her breath or straighten out her thoughts, "I have to think about it," she whispered, her eyes closed and her head leaned back into the pillows on the bed as his mouth moved slowly down her neck toward her collar bone and she moaned softly again.

He grinned at her and kissed her mouth. "That's my girl," he whispered, "My girl… my Jillian. Hold on to me." Obediently, she slowly slid her arms around his chest to his back as he lowered himself onto her body, pushing her legs apart with his and kissed her mouth, savoring every moment there.

"Wait, Anderson, I don't know if this is the right-" she started to say, but he leaned over and stopped her mouth with a deep kiss, and closed his arms around hers tightly as he moved his erection against her body, rubbing back and forth over the outside of her clothes, drawing the heat in her right to the surface and making her cry out softly. Then he lifted his mouth from hers and continued to rub himself firmly on her core as he spoke.

"It's right, baby, it's exactly right. I'm going to be your husband and your lover, for the rest of your life, and this is what lovers and husbands do. It's going to feel so good, and I'm going to do this with you all the time." His tone grew slightly husky and his mouth and hands became ravenous for her.

"It couldn't be more right," he said excitedly, rubbing himself against her more fervently as he kissed her mouth and neck. "It's poetic justice. Reed always got everything, got his way, got all the women, got whatever he wanted, and he was going to get the money, the business, the house, everything there was to get, everything he wanted, including you, and now that's all gone… and look what I get.

"I get it all because you broke it off with him and chose me. I get the money, the business, the house," he kissed her hard and hungrily, "I get the beautiful bride… the one woman in the world who doesn't want him, the woman he wants so much and can't have…" he laughed and grasped her breast, "I get to have a woman he hasn't ever had before, finally, I come first. I win."

She opened her eyes wide as she realized that the thing which had eluded her since they had first walked into the bedroom had finally clicked. She scooted out from under him. "Anderson! Stop!" she said, irritation flashing across her face. He sat up quickly and stared at her.

"What's wrong? What is it?" he asked, panic filling his voice.

She shook her head at him. "I haven't said yes, I haven't made up my mind about anything. I have no idea what I'm going to do, or who will or won't be a lover or husband of mine, and I certainly don't want to wind up becoming the prize of some ages old competition between the two of you! I might not marry either of you at all!"

Anderson looked worriedly at her for a moment and then pushed himself off the bed. He pulled his shirt back on, buttoning it up with his back to her. He took a deep breath and then finally turned and looked at her.

"Jillian, that isn't at all what's going on here. I'm your friend. I'm here to help you and support you. I just happen to be falling for you at the same time, and it wouldn't be the worst thing in the world if you really looked at Reed and I both and chose me to be your husband.

"You're entering into what amounts to an arranged marriage. I'm the better of the brothers and you have a choice. You could choose the one who wants you, who would treat you the best and give you the whole world." He walked toward her and slid his hands around her cheeks, cupping her face and lifting it toward him.

"You are an amazing woman, I know that and he doesn't. He couldn't care less who you are. I would cherish you. I would make your life wonderful. Please, just think about it," he said softly, lowering his face to hers and kissing her lips slowly, then opening his eyes and sighing as he let his hands fall away. He turned and looked over his shoulder at her. "We'll be landing soon; you need to buckle yourself in somewhere."

Chapter 6

Jillian was not looking forward to the conversation she was going to have to have with her mother. When she got home, she walked into her mother's office and sat down at her desk. Kimiko turned to look at her and her brow furrowed.

"Well? What is it? What's that look on your face?" she asked her daughter.

"The wedding is off, Mother," Jillian answered, her heart in her throat.

Her mother raised her chin and looked down her nose at her daughter for a long silent moment. "Why is the wedding off?"

"Because I have walked in on Reed having sex with another woman twice already, once right before he asked me to marry him and once yesterday," she answered shortly.

Her mother scowled at her. "You think you aren't going to marry him because he is having a good time with other women? Most men go and enjoy women outside of their marriage beds. It's natural. It's the way men are."

"Daddy doesn't do that to you," Jillian said quietly.

Kimiko didn't even blink. "Your father is a very rare man. All the same, it's not an issue that should prevent you from marrying Reed. It is an unacceptable break. You will marry him."

"Mother! I won't! I don't want to marry a man who won't be faithful to me!" Jillian spoke against her mother's wishes, which was something she almost never did.

Kimiko's eyes narrowed and she looked at her daughter for another long, silent moment. "You wish to be disobedient and dishonor your parents and your uncles; to go against our decisions for you?" She turned her chair toward the table behind her and picked a file up off of it. She turned back toward Jillian and placed it before her on her desk.

"This, dishonorable child, will be your future if you choose to disobey me and break your marriage agreement." Kimiko leaned back in her chair and folded her hands beneath her chin. "You will be sent to Japan immediately and you will live with your uncles there until your wedding day to the man in the file. He is the wealthy owner of a finance company in Japan. He has even more money than Carter's family does.

"Should you marry him, you will not see the United States again. You will be a Japanese citizen and you will live in that country for the rest of your life. You will have Japanese children, you will raise them with Japanese customs in a Japanese culture, and that is how you will live out all of your days."
Her mother leaned forward and looked at her with unblinking eyes. "Also, in case you are wondering, Japanese men have lovers on the side as well, and you will not be permitted to have an opinion about it."

Jillian opened the file and looked at the face of an old man with thin gray hair and the beginnings of liver spots on his face.

"Mother! How old is he?" Jillian asked, horrified.

"He is sixty-seven. Don't believe for a moment that he will die anytime soon and release you of your duty to him as his wife. The men in his family all lived to be over one hundred and ten years old." Her mother smiled at her with a shallow smile.

"So, you can see your two options and you can see that I have obviously chosen a better husband for you. He is a wealthy and attractive man. You could do much worse."

Jillian thought for a moment and looked at her mother. "What if there was an option you haven't considered yet?"

Kimiko frowned. "What option would that be?" she asked cynically.

"Well, Carter told Reed that if he didn't marry me, he would be disinherited and would be made to leave their home and their family. If that was to happen, Reed's younger brother Anderson would inherit everything and he would be running the company and handling the business. He has asked me to marry him. I could marry the younger brother and our families would still be united, you would still have the business opportunity you are hoping to create." Jillian held her breath, waiting for her mother's response.

She hadn't even decided for herself whether she would accept Anderson, whether or not Reed was still in the picture. He seemed somewhat jealous and greedy.

Kimiko shrugged. "I don't care which brother you marry. Talk to Carter about it and see what he has to say. Marry one of them. Do it soon. We are finished discussing this."

Jillian glanced back down at the old man in the photo of the file on her mother's desk. She wanted to believe that her mother was kidding and that she would never be married off to an old man in another country, but there he was, staring back from his photo at her, and she knew that her mother would indeed do such a thing. She walked out and closed the screen door of her mother's office behind her.

So she was to marry one of the brothers, but which one? She would go and talk to Carter as Kimiko had instructed. She might hate that she was being made to marry anyone at all, but her mother did have good advice. She walked to the garden and sat at the Koi pond, missing her father and wishing she had a little more control over her life.

A short while later, Kimiko slid the screen door of the house open and called to Jillian.

"You have a visitor!" she announced with a wide smile. Jillian looked up and saw Reed walking toward her, fully dressed, she noted, and she lowered her eyes and scowled as her mother closed the door with a warning look.

He walked up to Jillian and stopped before her. "May I speak with you, please?" he asked hopefully.

She nodded and walked to the bench beneath the tree, overlooking the koi. He sat beside her and his voice was soft as he spoke. "Jillian, I owe you an apology you should probably never accept, but I'm going to give it to you anyway, and I want to share some things with you that might help you hurt less."

She turned her head slightly toward him to indicate that she was listening, but she didn't look at him.

"Okay, I know I deserve that. Actually, I deserve much worse, but I just had to come and try to make this right with you. The girl that you saw me with both of those times, her name is Daisy. She is a stripper and she was a friend of mine for a long time. Well, not really so much as friend as a bed companion. I realized when you left the hotel that I have been using her to make myself feel good and doing nothing at all that's beneficial to her. I don't love her. I'm never going to love her. We aren't friends, we don't hang out, we don't have a relationship like that.

"I was just in it for the physical affection from a pretty girl, but that was selling her short, that was taking her for granted, using her, disrespecting her, and stealing away any chance she might have at real happiness with someone who might actually love her in ways that I never will. I realized how utterly selfish I've been over the time I've known her and I had to cut our ties and let her go. I couldn't keep using her like I have been, and I will be honest with you, lately the only thing I want her around for... uh... this is going to be tough." He ran his hand through his dark hair and the tousled locks fell into his eyes because he was looking down.

Jillian turned her gaze toward him finally, dumbfounded by the things he was saying to her. This did not sound anything like the man she had gotten to know over the last few weeks. Nothing at all like him. She watched him carefully, wondering what to believe.

"One thing you're going to learn about me, I hope, is that I'm honest. I don't always make the right decisions, but I am honest. Lying takes too much work. I can't ever remember the lies, so I just stick with what I know is true." He smiled at her. "In case you wondered."

He shifted uncomfortably and took a deep breath. "This is pretty embarrassing, so just hear me out, please. Something happened to me after I went on that date with you. You sort of... I guess you sort of saturated my brain and my heart, and I just couldn't get you out of my head. I normally wouldn't see Daisy that often, but I was trying to get you off my mind and I was using her as a distraction, trying to focus on her, but it backfired terribly."

He looked away from her as he spoke. He couldn't bear to look her in the eye. "I slept with her the day after our date, and when we were together, all I could think about was you. That day, when I was with her, when I was..." he nodded at Jillian and Jillian closed her eyes for a moment.

"I get it," she said quietly.

"When that was happening, all I could think of was you. I wanted you so much I wanted it to be you with me in that bed, and it was one of the most incredible experiences I've ever had; not because it was Daisy with me, but because I was imagining it was you with me... imagining that you wanted me as much as I wanted you. Well, I was mad as hell afterward that I had thought of you like that.

"You slapped me. You hated me. Why would I think of you that way? But then I couldn't get you out of my mind again and I asked you to come over to the house because Carter told me if I didn't ask you to marry me that I was going to lose everything; my family, my home, the business I was supposed to take over when he retires; all of it. So, I was up against a wall. Somehow, I had to figure out how to get a girl who hated me to marry me and I had one week to do it.

109

"I was so stressed out. So worried. I thought my whole life was over right then. Daisy had driven me home that morning and we were in the pool house. I went to take a shower and all I could think about was you. All I wanted was you. I just couldn't get you off of my mind, it drove me crazy.

"I got out of the shower and tried to use Daisy to distract me, to get you off my mind. But suddenly there you were again, when I closed my eyes. I pretended it was you I was with and then you walked in on me. I thought that was the end of the universe, but I had to ask you to marry me.

"I had to ask you to take the chance on me, and you did. I was serious about it. I mean, I am serious about it, but then Anderson sent me off to Vegas for my bachelor party and he arranged for Daisy to be there. Every time she touched me, all I wanted to do was pretend it was you. I'm so addicted to the thought of you; it's like I've inhaled you and nothing I can do will get you out of my system.

"I just can't get over you. It's why I was calling your name out when I was with her and you and Anderson walked in on us. I was pretending it was you beneath me, that it was you I was kissing. I needed you, and you hate me. That just became the closest I could get to you. She became my 'Jillian Substitute'. I realized after you left that I was using her and it was the most unfair thing I could ever have done. I told her the truth and broke it off with her; a clean break.

"I gave her money to go start a new life so she doesn't have to strip anymore and I told her I don't want to see her again. I hope she finds someone someday who will really love her, but I told her it was never going to be me."

He stopped and covered his face, then ran his hands through his hair. He was hoping that some of that made sense to Jillian, and he desperately hoped that he hadn't come across as an obsessed creep.

110

"Does Anderson know that you started liking me?" Jillian asked quietly. She was absorbing all he said, but his honesty, his confession and his genuine interest in her had made a significant change in her heart, though she wasn't sure she wanted him to know that yet.

"Yeah, I told him before the Vegas trip. He came to talk with me and asked me how I was feeling about you, asked if I was really serious about the marriage. He thought I might go off with Daisy and forget about you, but I told him how much I've been thinking about you and he was surprised."

Jillian's brow furrowed as she thought about the things that Anderson had said on the plane. "Would you say he's really competitive with you?" she asked curiously, knowing the side of him that she had seen was extremely competitive and also very sneaky and conniving.

Anderson had arranged for Reed and Daisy to go to Vegas after Reed admitted to wanting her and Anderson had taken Jillian to Vegas with him on purpose, so that she would see Reed with Daisy and break the marriage off so he could ask her to marry him without looking like he was butting in on his brother's girl.

It didn't justify Reed having intercourse with Daisy while he was engaged to Jillian; she solidly felt that never should have happened, but she could see that both of them wanted her, and they were both willing to do what it took to get her.

Her dark and sad world brightened slightly. She decided not to say anything to Reed just then about his brother trying to steal her away from him, as Reed seemed unaware of it.

Reed shrugged his shoulders. "He's not any more competitive than any other brother, I think. Why do you ask?"

He looked at her finally and felt his heart slow down and begin to untether itself from his body. He looked into her eyes and glanced at her lips, smiling, talking, saying something in her sweet voice. He lost himself in her, his heart freed itself from him and floated away to her, and she absorbed it, without ever even knowing it happened.

"Reed?" she asked, looking at him expectantly.

He shook his head a little. "I'm sorry, what did you say?"

She smiled at him sympathetically. "I asked you if you would like to try another date. Maybe we can figure out how to get along."

He almost jumped up from the bench. "Yes! Yes, please, let's go do... let's... um, what would you like to do? Anything you want to do would be perfect with me," he said with a big grin, settling back down on the bench beside her.

"I'll leave that to you." She smiled. "Tomorrow?"

"Yes. When can I pick you up and how long can I have you with me?" he asked, flashing a big grin.

She raised one eyebrow. "Okay, how about ten in the morning, and you can have me back whenever you are ready to bring me home."

His grin softened and he looked at her seriously. "I don't think your parents will let me keep you that long unless we're married."

Jillian blinked in surprise. "How about you have me back by ten tomorrow night?"

"I am going to give you the best day of your life," he promised, standing up and offering her his hand to help her up. "Thank you for talking with me. I appreciate it."

He paused, not sure if he should hug her or not, and she saw his hesitation and smiled, turning her cheek toward him. Reed gazed at her and time seemed to drift more slowly as he lifted his hands to cup her face.

He lowered his lips to her cheek and paused before they touched her skin, breathing her in and finding rapture in the closeness of her, and only then did he press his lips lightly to her cheek and linger there a moment before letting her go.

Her heart began to pound and she took a deep breath and smiled at him. "Till tomorrow morning then." He nodded and left her quietly in the garden.

The next morning he picked her up and asked her if she had gotten his message about what to wear and what to bring.

"I did. It's all packed in my bag here," she said with a smile. Her mother watched them with a pleased look on her face as they drove away.

"So, where are we going?" she asked him.

"I'm taking you out on the boat. I thought we'd have a nice time out on the water today, have a picnic on an island and lounge around, then watch the sunset and then I'll bring you back, after we've sailed under the stars for a little while." He smiled at her.

Jillian raised her eyebrows. "That sounds like a fun day. I hope it works out like that."

He took her to the yacht and she was dumbfounded with its splendor. He gave her the tour, showing her the lower deck where all the cabins, dining room, galley, bathrooms and the office and library were, and then he took her upstairs to the bridge and the deck. It was an enormous boat and she teased him that they could almost get lost on it. He said he had gotten lost on it more than once and she laughed at him.

He drove the boat out into the sea and placed a pretty white captain's hat on her head, telling her that she was official because of it. She laughed at him. They sailed for a while, dropped anchor and swam in the sea during the morning, swimming with turtles and dolphins, and in the far distance, they saw whales passing by.

After he let her shower first and change while he showered, and when he came back up to the deck, she caught her breath when she saw him with his wet hair and his sky blue eyes. He really was an incredibly beautiful man.

They stopped at a small deserted island and hauled lunch ashore so that they could play in the sand and lie under the umbrella and eat. Jillian said she couldn't remember when she'd had a better day, and Reed said he felt the same way.

"What would you be doing if your dad hadn't decided to make you marry me?" she asked him as they were walking through the surf side by side.

He shook his head and looked at the white and blue waves washing up on their feet, then up at her. "Honestly, I'd be ruining my life. I'd be out getting drunk, making poor life choices, and destroying my future. You really have saved me, you just don't realize it," he said, smiling at her and losing himself in her big dark brown eyes.

She smiled at him. "I'm beginning to realize it. Those changes are yours to make, though, whether I'm in the picture or not."

He stopped her and reached for her hand, holding it and closing his finger around it. "For the record, I really hope you're in the picture."

She laughed and smiled, but his words warmed her heart, and she felt closer to him than she ever had.

"What about you? What would you be doing if your parents hadn't forced you to be chained to me for eternity?"

She frowned and he saw it. "Uh-oh... something bad?"

Jillian looked away from him and then looked back at him. "I was already engaged to another man. His name was Wilson. I loved him with all my heart and we were going to be married, but my mother absolutely forbade me from seeing him ever again and then he called me and broke up with me. He said he found another woman he wanted to be with more than me and it was over. That happened right before I met you again. It was horrible."

He had stopped walking and was watching her, listening to her. "God, I'm so sorry. You sound like your whole life was already figured out and your parents just came in and changed the whole thing. That's horrible."

"Well, my Mother, not my father. Daddy would never make me do something I didn't want to do. I know the marriage was her idea. Carter is her business associate. Daddy isn't even part of it, really. He's off in Japan right now with my uncles. I miss him so much. I hope he comes home soon," she said sadly.

Reed saw her sad face and reached down into the waves and splashed her, drenching her in water. She gasped in shock for a moment and then the war was on. They splashed and screamed in delight as they chased each other and soaked each other, and she was ahead until a big wave came and she turned with a yelp and he dove for her, hollering, "I'll save you!"

When the water receded, she was on her back on the sand and he was on top of her, his arms wrapped around her. They laughed for a moment and then a serious look of longing came over his face as he gazed down at her, but then he touched his forehead to hers and closed his eyes, saying softly, "Thank you for spending the day with me." He started to lift himself off her, but she reached her hands to his shoulders and pulled him back down.

Reed looked at her carefully, and then she placed her hands on either side of his face and lifted her lips to meet his. He didn't close his eyes. His fantasy was finally real and he wanted to see all of it. Their lips met softly, sweetly, shyly for a moment, and then she kissed him again and tasted the sea on his lips.

He was incredibly tender with her, taking his time and moving over her mouth for long moments. Their bodies tensed and their fingers curled, as she reached around him to embrace him, holding him close to her. He tentatively opened her mouth with his tongue, tasting hers in gentle touches at first and then they lost themselves in the deepness of a passionate kiss.

When the moment came when they might take their exploration further or turn the moment light, he kissed her once more, softly, and lifted himself off her, pulling her up to him. She was surprised and pleased. She wouldn't have minded kissing him more at all, but he was the one who was careful not to go too far out of respect for her, and she loved that.

They went back to the boat after a while and showered again, then after the shower, he asked her what she'd like to do. It was still a while before sunset and he was open to suggestions.
"Well, honestly, we've played pretty hard today. I wonder if it would be alright to have a nap?" she asked with a shy smile. She was worried that she might be being rude. "It's not that I'm bored or anything, I just feel a little tired from all the fun and sun, that's all."

"Oh sure…" he teased her with a wink. "I'm supposed to believe that from the winner of the water fight?" He led her to the cabins downstairs and opened the door to the master suite.

She gave him a friendly shove. "Hey! Being a winner is tiring!" She walked into the room and looked at the bed gratefully. "Thanks, Reed," she said with a smile, still feeling guilty.

"No problem. I'll be upstairs when you wake up," he said with a smile, watching her as she climbed onto the bed. He wanted her desperately, but he would not let anything ruin their perfect day. She was worth fighting for and winning. She was worth everything, no matter what he went through.

She looked at him watching her. "Reed," she said softly, "You can come lay down with me to nap if you want to."

He paused a moment in the doorway, and then quietly closed the door and walked to the bed, crawling into it beside her. She snuggled into his arms and rested her head on his chest and in minutes, she

116

was sleeping. Reed could not sleep. He was wide awake in his daydream and he didn't want to miss a moment of it, but the salt, the sun, and the sea conspired against him and after a long while he fell asleep with her.

When he awoke, he saw that it was late in the afternoon, and Jillian was laying on his arm, looking at him. He smiled at her. "What is it, little fish?" he asked her, teasing her. "Didn't you get any sleep?"

She looked into his blue eyes and felt her heart being tugged away like it was drifting in a current, and there wasn't much she could do to struggle against it. She leaned up and looked at him solemnly and he watched her as she lowered her face to his and kissed him again.

His breath was stolen immediately and he gasped, pulling her on top of him and wrapping his arms around her. She kissed him in moments, learning him, tasting him, wondering at the electric butterflies that began to move through her body as he kissed her back, his arms tight around her, his tongue sliding over hers as he tried desperately to hold back his passion, so as not to overwhelm her.

He was surprised when her curious passions led her to sit up and bring him up with her, so that she could unbutton his shirt, one shy, brave button at a time, until she was looking at his bare chest and he was looking at her, waiting to see what she wanted to do. She held her breath as she pushed his shirt off his shoulders and slid it down his arms. He pulled his hands out of it and cupped her face with them, kissing her gently at first, and then he let her feel some of the hunger for her that coursed through him. She laid back down on the bed and pulled him on top of her.

He was amazed, incredulous that she would want him that way, that close and he closed his arms around her and kissed her mouth like it was the only nourishment that might keep him alive. His breath came rapid and short, and hers was quickly growing shallow as well. Heat built between them, as did need, and it was evident between them both in no time.

The feel of his skin beneath her hands was warm and soft and it felt comforting to her. Her body was reacting strongly to his attentions, his soft slow kisses and his hot tongue as he lowered his mouth from her lips to her neck and from there to the top curve of her breast. He began kissing her dark flesh tenderly, tasting and sucking as he moved his hand beneath her breast and slowly, carefully, slid it up over the soft full curve, gently squeezing it and moving his thumb over her hardening nipple that was straining for his touch through the thin material of the top of her dress.

He was touching what he had only imagined and it was a precious surreal dream for him. She slid her legs around his and he could not hide his hardened desire from her as he laid snuggly between her thighs. She gasped and her eyes flew open, but just then, he pressed his erection solidly in between her thighs and began to rub it firmly against her body through her gauzy sundress. She cried out involuntarily as the totally unfamiliar sensation of desire swept through her and she arched her back and drew in her breath as deeply as she could, closing her eyes to try to get a hold of herself.

He groaned in need at the feel of her body reacting to his.

Reed saw her reaction and his hand paused in its place on her breast. He watched her carefully and pressed his erection hard to her core again, rubbing the bulge of it back and forth over her clothes, pushing solidly against her, and watching her face. Her eyes flew open and she looked at him partly in panic and partly in wonder, and he smiled slowly and stopped for a moment.

"My sweet little Jillian…" he whispered to her, "would I be correct in guessing that you are a virgin?" He could not hide the pleased surprise on his face.

She turned her head away and bit her lip, lowering her lashes. He chuckled and turned her head back to face him. She opened her eyes and looked up at him, embarrassed.

"Oh Jillian, don't feel bad about that. Not at all." He chuckled again and grinned as he pressed his erection against her again and began to rub himself on her core slowly and deliberately, making her gasp and cling to his shoulders.

"I didn't think I could want you more than I did a minute ago," he said huskily, "but now there's no way I'm letting you go." He closed his mouth over hers and kissed her deeply and hungrily as his hand squeezed her breast firmly and he continued to move his body against hers. She was reeling with desire, and hormones were blazing through her as she tried to find some sort of stronghold in the ocean of chaos swirling throughout her.

Reed's hunger for her seemed to multiply infinitely then, and his hands and mouth moved over her more rapidly, needing her much more than he had before he discovered she had never known another lover, but then he paused and stopped and she looked at him quickly.

"Wait," he said breathlessly, "I don't want to go too fast with you. You need to be ready for your first time. You need to really want it, and it needs to be with someone who means a great deal to you. It can't happen because of lust. I won't do that to you," he said quietly, his heart pounding as he gazed down at her, needing her with every fiber in his body, and denying himself completely as he put her first.

She saw what he was doing, and it brought a tear to her eye. "When did I begin to matter to you?" she asked him as her heart swelled with emotion.

He looked at her without blinking. "When you slapped me for disrespecting you. I never should have made you feel like you needed to defend yourself."

She smiled and the tear rolled down her cheek. He leaned down and kissed it away.

"Reed," she said softly. "Make love with me, please. I want you. I can't believe, it but I want you so much." Her voice dropped to a whisper. "Be my first love."

He stared at her for a long moment. "No one could be more surprised than me," he said quietly. "I'm honored." He kissed her softly and then pulled her up off of the bed and she looked at him in surprise, until he took her in his arms and kissed her, holding her closely before taking a step back and slowly, carefully unbuttoning her sundress, and as each button fell away, his lips kissed her flesh and tasted her.

The dress finally dropped to the floor. He slipped her bra from her, taking his time and enjoying every moment of it. His fingertips moved delicately over her curves, touching every part of her, feeling her, uncovering her, discovering her, arousing her, and setting her skin on fire where he had touched her.

"You are so much more beautiful than I ever imagined." He said it quietly, taking her into his arms again so she could feel his body against hers. She closed her eyes, amazed at the sensations it brought her.

He lowered her onto the bed and starting at the base of her legs, kissed her from her ankles all the way to her inner thighs, where he pushed her legs apart and pressed his lips and tongue to her, tasting her, drinking her in deeply, and making her moan in amazement and happiness.

"Reed!" she cried out as he made her come for the first time with his tongue. "What is that? What's happening?"

He smiled. "That's your first orgasm, my love. I'm going to give you so many of those today that you will lose count."

He had that accomplished before he kissed her there a final time and moved his ravenous mouth up her body to her breasts. It was there that he had to stop and gaze down at her. Her beautiful long black veil of hair was splayed out beneath her, just as he had imagined, her dark skin soft and warm, her nipples hard and anxious for him, and her mouth smiling up at him, her dark brown eyes looking at him in adoration. He was choked up for a moment and she placed her hands on his face.

120

"What's the matter?" she asked him, worried.

"It's just that looking at you, lying beneath me like this; I'd swear I was dreaming, but I know that can't be, because you never looked this incredible in my dreams." He shook his head and smiled down at her and then lowered his mouth to hers and kissed her with all the passion of a lover whose hunger is evergreen.

His hands closed over her breasts, as did his tongue and his mouth, and then when she didn't realize it was going to happen, he entered her and the momentary sharp pain of girlhood slipping away into womanhood made her clutch him, and he kissed her as it happened. He kept kissing her as he moved within her, loving her, bringing her unimagined pleasure, until she came for him again. This time it was because he was her lover, and was deep inside of her, while their lips were sharing heat and breath and desire.

She sighed in exquisite ecstasy as it washed over her and her whole body stiffened beneath his. He paused for her, waiting a moment, and when it passed, she had learned passion. He continued to move himself inside of her, bringing her to the hilt of bliss, and as she was reaching another climax, he said into her ear, "I love you, Jillian, marry me. Marry me for love, not because we were told to, but because you want to be with me for the rest of your life, just as I want to be with you."

She said yes, over and over again, yes. He made love to her for hours, until at last he could no longer hold himself back and he pushed himself as far into her as he could, and she felt his orgasm fill her with fire. She came again, and then they collapsed in love and exhaustion, and slept in each others arms.

Chapter 7

Reed and Jillian were blissfully happy, and he had her back at her house by ten that evening, but neither one wanted to say goodbye. He opened her car door and helped her out, pulling her into a hug and kissing her neck and her mouth before she turned to walk into the house, but she didn't get two steps before she stopped in her tracks and felt as though her heart was going to explode.

"Jillian…" he called her name.

Their eyes met as he walked toward her. "Wilson!" she said in shock and Reed's hands closed firmly around her shoulders in protection.

"What on earth are you doing here?" she asked in confusion, pain searing through her heart at having to see him.

He walked toward her until he was just a few steps in front of her. "God, you look so beautiful. I've missed you more than you can imagine." He sighed and looked behind her shoulder at Reed, then back down to her. Reed eyed the tall physically fit young black man before him, and he felt his heart pound against his chest in panic that this man might actually be able to take away the woman he was holding.

"I have to tell you something." He said with a dejected voice. "I'm not proud of it. Far from it, but I just have to change it. I have to get you back. I can't live without you, baby."

"You *left me for another woman*!" Jillian cried out, pain and anger surging through her. "What do you mean, you can't live without me? You chose to live without me!"

Wilson reached his hand toward her, and then pulled it back. "Well, that's not exactly true," he said quietly, then looked down at the ground. "I'll tell you the truth. The truth is," he looked back up into her eyes, "there is no other woman. There never was another woman. You were my only woman. You were the one I wanted to marry and spend my whole life with, but then one day I got this phone call; I thought it was you, see, because it was your phone number, but when I answered it, I found out that it was your mother on the phone."

He turned and looked back at her house behind him, and then looked at her again. "Your mother said you had this great opportunity for a better life, that you had things you had to do that were bigger and better than me, and that I was holding you back and if I really loved you, I would tell you that I found another woman and tell you I wanted to break it off with you.

"She said that would be the real test of love, letting you go to move on with your life so I wasn't holding you back. I didn't want to hold you back from anything.

"I love you, baby, I always wanted to see you do good and have the best. So I told your mother that I loved you plenty, but how did she know that I wasn't the best thing for you, and then she said she'd give me one hundred thousand dollars if I told you about the other woman and broke up with you like she wanted me to.

"Well, it was a lot of money, so I did it. I called you back up and I lied to you. I told you that there was another woman, but there never was. I lied to you to set you free," he said, looking like he'd just delivered a heart wrenching poem.

Jillian slapped him straight across the face. Reed almost felt sorry for Wilson, having been on the receiving end of one of her slaps before. "You *lied* to me? You lied to me for money?"

"I'm sorry, baby. I don't care about the money no more. That rich guy can have it back. I just want you." Wilson nodded at Reed.

"What do you mean the rich guy? What are you talking about?" she asked, pulling herself away from Reed and looking at them both.

Wilson nodded at Reed, indicating him. "This is the guy, Reed, who your mother wants you to marry, isn't it?" he asked.

"Yes," Jillian answered coldly.

"Well, Reed and his dad Carter are the ones that came up with the money that your mother paid me off with. They was all working together to keep us apart and hook you up with him, and I guess it worked, if he's standing in your yard hanging on you."

Reed stepped into the conversation at that point. "I didn't know anything about a payoff. Don't drag my name into your mess. Whatever Carter and Kimiko did is between them, and I'm not involved."

Wilson puffed his chest out defensively. "You calling me a liar? I know what you did. I know you gave the money to Jillian's mother, she told me you did, *Reed*."

Reed started to argue with him, but Jillian put her hands up in the air to stop them both. "You two both need to leave my house right now. I'm done talking to both of you. This is over. Now! Out!"

They both turned to look at her, each one thinking that she would let him stay, and she raised her voice to both of them. "Get out! Both of you!"
They both backed away from her, each one walking to his car and staring at her before getting into their cars and driving away. Jillian walked into the house and slammed the front door, which was the only American door in the house.

"Mother!" she yelled.

Kimiko appeared from her bedroom and had a look of sheer fury on her face, but when she saw the expression on Jillian's face, she paused and turned her head to the side a little. "What is it?"

Jillian almost growled at her. "You paid my fiancé off with one hundred thousand dollars so I would be forced to marry Reed? You sacrificed my future and my happiness for your business?

124

"Do I mean anything to you at all? Anything? How dare you treat me like I'm a marketable product! I am your daughter! It should be my choice to marry whom I want to marry and my decision as to when I want to get married, just like you did with Daddy.

"Don't try to come talk to me until I'm ready to speak with you, because I have nothing to say to you!"

Jillian walked away from her mother and then stopped and turned to glare at her. "The wedding is off. I'm not marrying either of Carter's sons and I'm not going to Japan to marry that old man. I'm not getting married. I'm closed for business!"

Chapter 8

Jillian was beyond mere anger. Her heart was distraught at being lied to by her mother, by Wilson, the man she had intended to marry for love and her own first choice for a life mate, and both Carter and his son Reed.

 She'd discovered that they had all been lying to her and she wasn't speaking to any of them. She told her mother not to bother trying to talk to her;it was an act of tremendous disrespect, and she knew it, but she spoke her heart for once and because she had never spoken to her mother that way in her life, her mother had not said anything to her in return. Kimiko had given her the space that she had demanded and it had given her a little room to breathe and think.

She sorely wished that her father could have been home for her just then. He always seemed to know the best way to see her through her grief, but he was away in Japan working with her uncles and his trip had already been postponed.

 He talked with her over the Internet, but he was not there to hold her and help her through her grief and pain. A day after she had found out, Wilson was back at her front door trying to talk to her, but she wouldn't see him.

She refused to discuss anything with him, and he seemed determined not to give up on her. He began sending frequent notes to her, begging her to give him some time so that he could explain, but she would not relent. Reed did the same, sending her flowers and trying to call her. She was impenetrable. She would not respond to any of their endeavors.

Reed was beside himself with anxiety for many reasons. More than anything, the seed of love had just begun to bud and grow between them and suddenly it was ripped away. It caused an unfamiliar sensation in him; a pain in his heart that he had never known. He had loved many women physically, but he had never loved a single woman with his heart, and heartache was an entirely new experience for him.

He had no idea how to handle it, what to do to fix what had been broken in him and between them, or how to win her back and he most assuredly wanted her back. He needed her back. He began to realize that as he laid in his bed night after night, alone and longing for her, unable to sleep because thoughts, doubts, memories and second guesses plagued him. Her silence was deafening to him and it did nothing to help his worries.

He was hoping for help when he walked into his brother's office the morning after, to seek some advice. He and Anderson were not exactly close, but he thought if anyone knew how to get over a broken heart, surely his brother would. He knew Anderson had lousy luck with women and must be well versed at recovering a bruised and tattered relationship. Reed sat down at Anderson's desk and his brother looked up at him with an almost impatient look on his face.

"I'm very busy, Reed, what is it?" he asked in a quiet tone.

Reed leaned forward and rested his elbows on his knees and his chin in his hands. "I'm in some new territory and I wondered if you could help me out with it. I'm hoping you have some experience you could share with me."

"What is it?" Anderson repeated.

"Jillian and I were doing very well, but I guess her mother bought off her ex-fiancé and she found out about it when the guy showed up last night to tell her all about it and try to win her back. She told him off, but the guy told her that I was part of it and Jillian told me off, believing him, and now I can't get her to talk to me. I sent her flowers and I've tried to call her, but nothing is working. She won't talk to me at all." Reed was staring into his own nothing as he spoke, but as he finished he looked up to see that Anderson had suddenly given him his full attention.

Anderson leaned forward, his hand on his desk. "Reed, I'm so glad that you came to me with this. Explain to me how things were going with Jillian. Tell me the details. It will help me to know how best to handle this."

Reed stretched and rested his back on the chair. "Well, we went out on a great date and we really patched up the awkwardness between us. She had been really upset about Las Vegas, but she and I talked and I did my best to explain that I was just playing and that I really want to be with her. She understood and I can't believe it myself, but she believed me and we had an amazing time together. Now it's ruined over a lie.

"I didn't know anything about money that her mother gave to that guy she was already engaged to. I just know Carter told me to marry her or he was going to give the inheritance, the house, the business, all the assets, everything, to you. I couldn't be kicked out. I made her my priority and I found out, when I did that, that she is an incredible lady. Now I am developing feelings for her."

He looked right at his brother who was watching him like a hawk. "I have to tell you, Anderson, I think I'm falling in love with her. I really do. I've never felt like this before."

Anderson was silent until Reed finished, and then he took a deep breath and stood up and walked to the bar in his office and poured them each a stiff drink.

He walked over to Reed and handed him one of them. "Here. Drink this." Then he sat beside his brother and spoke to him. "What did she say to you when you saw her last?" he asked.

"She told me she didn't want me to talk to her, she didn't want to see me, and to leave her alone," Reed replied glumly.

"Then, dear brother," Anderson said, "listen to the woman. Give her the space and time she asked for. It's the least you can do. She's been overrun with emotions and confusion, she has been lied to and used. She's been told she had to marry someone she didn't know and doesn't like very well, and now, just as things have begun to shape up for her, the bottom has suddenly fallen out. She has been handed a truth that she has to figure out how to cope with.

"Don't go after her right now. Don't chase her and make it more difficult. She's had so much to deal with. Just give her some time and space. It really is what she needs. Stop calling her, stop sending her things, just leave her alone and let her have some time. Give it a few weeks and then get in touch with her if you haven't heard from her by then.

"My guess is that she will be in contact with you before too long. Her mother is fairly bent on her getting married and she won't let her daughter sit on her hands too long. I'm sure she'll be in touch with you soon. Until then, the best thing you can do is give her what she asked for. Give her time and space. Got that?"

Reed looked miserable. "Alright. I will. I'll wait for her to get in touch with me." He stood up, swallowed the remains of the whiskey in his glass and set the tumbler on Anderson's desk, then clapped his brother on the shoulder. "Thanks for the advice, brother." Then he strolled out of the room and sighed to himself.

Needs a separator

Jillian was sitting in her father's dojo when a knock sounded at the door. It surprised her, because it was rare that an interruption came at that place; it was a place of meditation and spiritual and physical focus.

"Yes?" she asked.

Her mother responded. "Jillian, you have a guest."

"Who is it?" she asked suspiciously.

In answer, the door slid open and she found herself looking at her mother and Anderson. He bowed low to her mother and let himself in. Kimiko smiled at him and nodded, then disappeared. He slid the screen closed behind him, then turned to look at Jillian.

"Hello." He smiled and started walking toward her.

She stood up from her seat on the mat beneath her and greeted him with a hug. He wrapped his arms around her and pulled her close to him, nestling his face in close to her neck and ear. He kissed her cheek softly and held his lips there for a lingering moment before letting her go and looking down at her.

"I've heard about what happened with Reed and Wilson and I wanted to come and be some support and help to you if I can. You must be so upset. How awful for you to have found out what you did, especially when you did. How are you feeling about it?" An outpouring of sympathy was flushing over his face as he reached for her hands.

Jillian turned her head away from him. "It makes me sick. I am so angry about it, and so sad. All this time I believed Wilson when he told me he had found someone else to love but it wasn't true. He said he's loved no one but me the whole time and that my mother paid him off. I wanted to marry him. I wanted to love him the rest of my life, but now I am so confused and hurt, I don't know who to believe or what to do," she said as an angry tear fell down her face while she tried to hold her emotions in check.

Anderson slowly wiped the tear away from her cheek with his fingertip and, noticing a curtained area with dozens of thick pillows on it, motioned for her to sit on the deeply cushioned resting platform with him. Her father used it for naps sometimes, as it was quiet and peaceful in his dojo. He had created a meditation section at one end of his dojo and a curtained area with a small waterfall and the resting cushions at the other end of it. She walked over with Anderson to the area and as they entered it, Anderson reached over and closed the curtains behind them, then lowered himself to the cushioned platform and sat close to Jillian.

He lifted his hand to her cheek and began to stroke it gently. "Jillian," he said softly, "Wilson couldn't have really loved you. If he had, then no amount of money would ever have been enough to keep him away from you. I understand that it was one hundred grand. That's not much money at all. Perhaps it seemed like it to him, but in the grand scheme of things, it's just not much money.

"He traded your love for that pittance, and it was worth it to him. For him to come around now and say that he wants you and that he is ready to give the money back, well, that just shows that he may have realized an inkling of what he had in you when he did have you." He continued. "You are worth so much more than that. You are worth being loved, really and truly being loved for the rest of your life, by someone who wouldn't trade anything at all for you. You are also worth more than being traded in marriage for a business deal, which is exactly what my brother is doing to get you.

He was threatened with being kicked out of our home, with losing his entire inheritance, the family business, which would go to him, and all the assets my father has. All of it was going to be taken away from him if he didn't marry you. That's the most important thing to him." He paused for dramatic effect and Jillian felt her heart turn over in her chest. She turned to look at him with wide, disbelieving eyes.

"That can't be true!" she gasped as the heartache in her was ripped open and fresh pain spilled out into her again.

"It's true. I'm so sorry my beautiful girl." Anderson wrapped his arm around her and pulled her close to him, holding her against him as tears began to fall down her cheeks again. He let her cry against his chest for a moment, and then he looked down at her face and said quietly, "I probably shouldn't share this with you, I feel like I'm betraying my own flesh and blood... my own brother.... But I just can't stand to see you hurting like you are, and you should know that..." He trailed off and looked away from her for a long moment.

She held her breath and said, "What?" but he kept his head turned. She reached her hand to his chin and turned his face toward her.

131

"What? Please, tell me!" she begged, hoping that she wouldn't regret asking. She wasn't sure she could take any more pain.

He reached up to her hand on his cheek and placed his hand over it, holding it there. "I just can't keep anything from you, my sweet Jillian, so I will betray my brother's trust and tell you this. He was just in my office this morning telling me that he is desperate to get you back so that he can marry you and inherit everything and stay in the house.

"There. I've said it. I feel horrible for letting him down and speaking the truth to you, but all he's interested in is the money and the business. That's all that's important to him. He told me that he managed to trick you into thinking that things were going really well between you two, that he made you believe he was falling for you. He even laughed about it."

Jillian felt as though her heart was being ripped right out of her chest through her ribs.

"He laughed, my darling, and it made me so sick to think that he is using you just to get to the money and the business. How could anyone who has someone as beautiful and incredible as you even think of using you and hurting you?

"I'm so sorry to have to tell you this horrible truth. I'm so sorry. On top of everything else, but I just had to."

Jillian could not hold the back the tears. She wept and he put both of his hands on her cheeks and pulled her face close to his, looking into her eyes awash with tears.

"I have to admit this to you, Jillian, I have to tell you the truth. I can't hold it back from you any longer. My feelings for you are so strong. You're all I think about, you are all I want. I can't keep you off of my mind... out of my dreams... and there's nothing I can do to stop it, but you have stolen my heart.

"I stand back and watch my brother hurt you time and time again, and he has, by screwing other women behind your back and lying to you, by working with your mother to buy off your ex-fiancé and force you into a marriage for business, but my love, I can no longer stand back and watch him do this. I just can't stand to see you hurt and used like they are using you. You don't deserve it. You deserve love. Real love. You deserve my love. You deserve someone who will always be there for you, to hold you and love you."

Jillian's emotions were raging. How had Reed managed to trick her so fully? How had she ever believed that he was developing feelings for her? She had given herself to him! She had let him be the first and only man to make love with her. She had believed that he wanted to be with her because he was beginning to love who she was, not because he was in it for the money! He had lied to her again! She was blown apart.

As she wept, Anderson's words found their way through to her and she looked up at him in surprise. He didn't speak again, instead, he leaned toward her and pressed his lips against hers, kissing her softly. He was tentative at first, careful, kissing her gently, and at first she didn't respond, but then he began to press his mouth to hers more fervently, and in all her anguish, she let him, and as his mouth opened hers and his tongue touched hers, she kissed him back. He pulled her tight against him.

His kiss deepened and his hands moved from her face to the back of her neck and her shoulder. She felt confusion, pain and sadness crashing through her like a torrent and his kiss seemed like some kind of strange anchor holding her in place in the middle of all of it.

Anderson kissed her lips and tasted her tongue, and then his mouth traveled over her cheek to her ear. "I want you, Jillian, I want you to be my wife. I've asked you before and I'm going to ask you again. You should be with me always. You would be loved. You would never need for anything. I can give you the world, my dear, I can give you everything.

133

"Both our parents would be pleased and you would have everything your heart could want. You'll fall in love with me in no time. You'll see. I can love you like no one ever has, and it won't ever go away." He whispered against her ear and her neck as he left little kisses on her skin.

His mouth found hers again, kissing her deeply as he carefully laid her back into the pillows and moved himself above her. She looked up at him in surprise and worry and he kissed her slowly and gently as he whispered to her, sliding his hands along her arms.

"Let me love you, my girl, let me take all the pain away. I can make it disappear in just a few minutes, and with every kiss I will drive it away. Let me take all your pain and sorrow away, beautiful girl, let me give you love, let me show you how strong it will be between us."

She was still crying from the news he had told her about Reed. He kissed her tears away and warmed her with his embrace, his arms close around her and his lips covering hers as his kisses grew hungrier. He opened her mouth with his and tasted her, and at first, she kissed him back, his tongue tracing hers, but then she stopped.

"I can't... I'm not sure what I want to do," she replied sadly.

He kissed her again. "I can help you. Let me take away your pain. Let me love you." His mouth was warm and wet on hers, insistent and demanding as his tongue explored hers and after a few long moments, she kissed him back. His mouth tasted like her salt tears and he was tender and careful with her. His erection pressed against her made it clear that he wanted her and that he wanted her to want him. She felt like everything in her was clouded and confused, found and lost all at once.

His hand moved to her blouse and he began to unbutton it, fingers moving swiftly over the buttons and uncovering her flesh. His mouth trailed down her neck to the generous curve of her breasts and his hand cupped one of her breasts. He moaned in need as he gently pushed her legs apart with his and pressed his solid erection against

134

her body, rubbing it back and forth over her thin skirt. She gasped at the hard feel of him on her and her body warmed slightly.

Moving his hand from her breast to her knee, he slid his fingers up underneath the material of her dress and along her skin until she reached down and stopped his hand just as he reached the middle of her thigh. He pressed his erection firmly against her again, rubbing the hardness of his desire against her body and kissing her mouth to stoke the flames of need within her. She kissed him in return, but she felt uncertain about what they were doing.

He tried to move his hand further up her thigh and she held him fast where he was. "What is it, my girl?" he whispered, looking down at her through eyes drunk with desire.

The problem was that what he was doing did not give her the same fire and need that Reed's hands and body and lips had given her. Anderson did not make her breathless and make her heart pound. Her body was warm, but it was nothing compared to what she had discovered in Reed's arms, and she knew that Reed's touch was what she really wanted.

"I'm not ready for this with you," she said quietly. "I'm sorry."

He pulled his hand from beneath her skirt and gently touched her cheek. "It's because you hurt," he said softly. "It's because you are confused and in pain. Let me help you, let me show you love. Let me make it better for you." He lowered his mouth to hers and moved his hand slowly from her cheek to her breast as his tongue twisted with hers in a determined kiss.

His fingers slid beneath her blouse and her bra and he felt her warm full breast with his hand, rubbing his fingers over her hard nipple and pressing his erection against her body again, rubbing it slowly on her, in an attempt to arouse and stimulate her. His mouth left hers and moved to her nipple, his tongue tracing it and moving strongly over it before he sucked it into his mouth and nibbled at it.

She let him for a moment, wondering if he could make the cold darkness in her disappear, but his amorous touches and kisses could not warm her and she knew it should not continue.

"No, Anderson. I'm really not ready. You might be right, and maybe someday I might be able to feel for you what you feel for me, but this is not that day," she said with sadness.

He paused in his kissing and looked at her. She saw a wall go up between his hunger for her and his face and he suddenly looked very business-like. He sat up and buttoned her blouse back up and then pulled her up into a sitting position and held her face, looking into her eyes.

"I'll wait for you to love me. I don't mind waiting at all. I'm going to keep trying; I can't let you go, though, so let's not give up on each other. Marry me. Say that you'll marry me, and then you and I will find a way to love each other over time. I will wait for you. Just say that you'll marry me now.

"Let me take you away from your mother and give you a new home at least. We'll work toward the love. I'll wait until you are ready. I'll give you anything you need, however you need it," he said, looking deeply into her eyes.

"I need a friend. I need an honest, good, loyal, loving friend," she said, her heart hopeful that she might have found one.

"I can do that," he replied, kissing her mouth, then looking at her with a smile. "I can be the best friend you ever had. And you should marry your best friend." He laughed a little and she laughed lightly with him.

She smiled finally and looked back at him. "I'll take it into serious consideration. Honestly, you are probably the best option I have right now for marriage." She laughed a little, but not much.

"I hope so. I'll be waiting." Then he kissed her again, long and slow, and she kissed him back. He stood up and held out his hand. "Would you like to come with me today and spend some time with me?"

She took his hand and stood up. "Actually, I really need some time alone today. Could you let me have a little time please?"

Anderson stood up and pulled her into a close embrace. "Of course. I will always give you anything you need." He smiled at her and let her go. "I'll see you soon. Please call me if you need anything at all, even if it is just to talk. Okay?" He widened his eyes at her to make his point.

"I will," she said with a smile back and then she closed the screen behind him and tried to still the chaos in her mind. She was meditating alone for no more than an hour when there was another knock on the door. She opened her eyes and sighed, then rose to open the screen and was shocked to see Wilson standing there.

"What are you doing here?" she asked in amazement.

He placed his hands on the frame of the screen door and looked at her desperately. "I need to talk with you! Please, just listen to me for a few minutes, that's all I ask!" he begged.

She scowled at him. "I told you I didn't want to hear from you ever again! I meant it!" She moved to close the door and he stopped her, holding it open with his hands and one of his feet.

"Please, Jillian, I have to talk with you. Just listen to me for a minute!" he almost pushed his way in and she finally stepped back and let him come into the dojo. He let go a deep breath and looked at her with wide, anxious eyes.

"I would never, ever do anything to hurt you. You have to know that. Your mother called me the morning we broke up and she used your phone when she did it, so at first I thought it was you, but then she started talking and she told me that you had this great opportunity to be with that guy, Reed.

137

"She said you were going to marry him, that you wanted to be with him and that I was being selfish and holding you back. She said she would give me a hundred grand if I just broke up with you that day and told you that I found someone else so that you wouldn't try to get me back."

He took a few steps closer to her. "Jillian, she said I didn't have anything to offer you, you know, that I come from the wrong side of the tracks and that you would have no future with me. I thought she was right, because... well, I don't really have anything to give you except my love."

Jillian felt nothing but anger rising in her. "Wilson, you had me. We had a future together, or so I thought, and I knew you didn't have much, but that never bothered me. I thought you loved me and that was enough for me!"

He reached for her, his dark hand closing around her arm. "I do love you! That's why I'm here! Don't you see? I just can't live without you. I love you. I want to spend the rest of my life with you! I told your mother she could keep the money and I will give every cent of it back to her. I was so miserable after I did that... after I made that mistake. I'm so sorry, baby."

She yanked her arm from his grasp. "You don't love me, Wilson. If you did, you never would have taken the money. You would have kept me no matter what. You wouldn't have lied to me, you wouldn't have hurt me, and you wouldn't have let me go right into the arms of another man. You knew that's where I was headed and you practically pushed me there.

"Don't you dare say you loved me. That money was worth more to you than our love. I hope you enjoy spending it, because it's the price of our love and our future. Now, I don't know how you got into this house, but I want you out. Now." She fumed at him.

He wouldn't budge. "I'm not leaving until you give me a chance, Jillian. I'm here, I love you, and I want you back. Please, for the sake of what we had, please give me a chance. I want you to remember all that we had," he said, reaching for her again and pulling her into his arms.

He planted his lips on hers and kissed her hard for a long moment, and in that moment, all the pain that she had felt when he told her he had found another love turned to anger, and the anger seemed to catch fire. She felt it begin to burn through her and as it did, the pain vanished. She shoved him away from her and he looked at her with pleading eyes.

"Jillian!" he called out desperately.

"You said you wanted another woman; that you loved someone else. Well now, you have the freedom to go make that lie a truth. Get out of here and don't ever come back. I never want to see you again." Her voice was almost cold and her eyes steely as she looked at him. He stared back at her, speechless, and she walked to the screen and opened it, looking at him meaningfully.

Wilson bowed his head and walked quietly out of the door, and she followed him until he was out of her house and the front door was closed behind him. Then she walked into the garden and sat beneath the tree by the pond in her favorite spot. She couldn't believe that Wilson had come to try to get her back, unbidden, and that he had chosen her mother's money over her.

What value did that make her? None. It made her worth nothing. It made her love worth nothing, and she was furious with him for what he had broken between them, but she was also somewhat relieved and learning what she had really meant to him before it was too late and she had married him.

Her thoughts turned to Reed and their strange and wild relationship. She had been forced into marrying someone she didn't like, and over the course of time together, she had discovered things about him that she did like. Those little things led her to feelings that warmed her, that made her feel as she never had before, and she had been foolish enough to follow those feelings and allow Reed to lay her down in his bed and make love with her.

She had given him her virginity, her innocence and youth. She had believed that there was something strong and beautiful building between them, and then she found out from Wilson that Reed had been in the arrangement with her mother the whole time; that he was aware that they were paying off her fiancé so that Reed could have her.

Jillian sat in bitterness for a moment until she realized that Wilson had willingly lied to her for the money he had gotten, and it was possible, however slightly, that he may have lied about more than just the money. He did seem desperate to get her back, and maybe he was desperate enough to lie to her so that he could have a chance at it.

She knew there was only one person who would tell her the truth if she asked, and that person was right in her own home. She took a deep breath and swallowed her anger then walked to her mother's office and knocked on the door.

"Come in," her mother answered in a cool tone.

Jillian entered and sat at her mother's enormous wooden Japanese styled desk. "Hello, Mother." She spoke quietly.

Her mother looked at her through narrowed eyes. "What is it that you need?" she asked.

"I have to know the truth about something, Mother. When you called Wilson and told him you'd pay him to stay away from me, when you told him to tell me that he had fallen in love with another woman, did you say anything to him about Reed? Was Reed in on the offer that you made? Was he a part of it?" She looked at her mother and tried not to show the anxiousness in her heart.

Her mother leaned back in her chair and looked silently at her daughter for a moment. "I did tell him that you had another prospect, and that it was a good one for you. I told him you had an obligation to your family that would give you a much better future than he could ever offer you, and that if he cared for you even in the slightest that he would let you go. I expected him to say no.

"I expected him to tell me that he loved you and that no amount of money could keep him away from you. That's what someone who was truly in love would have said. He took the money immediately, which showed me that he never had any real love for you. As for Reed, he had no part in my offer. He never knew anything about it.

"You see, I called Wilson when we were at tea that day, because I hadn't realized that you were as serious about him as you told me you were that day, and as soon as I found out what you were thinking, I acted to change it so that he wouldn't get in the way of our plans for you." Kimiko finished speaking and watched her daughter silently.

Jillian felt a rush of happiness and regret flood through her. She knew then that Reed was telling her the truth when he said he knew nothing about it. He had no part in it. Her heart soared. "Thank you, Mother," she said quietly, then stood and walked out of the office, closing the door behind her.

She took her mother's car to Reed's house and was relieved when he answered the door. He took one look at her and pulled her into his warm, close embrace immediately. She was never so glad to see him as she was at that moment.

She looked up at him and tears began to fill her eyes. "Reed, I found out the truth. I'm so sorry I didn't believe you. I just found out that you had nothing to do with Wilson and with my mother's bribe to him. I'm so very sorry-" she started to say, but he only smiled down at her in his arms and whispered, "No apologies. None." And he covered her mouth with his, kissing her softly, his hands holding her face and stroking her long glossy black hair.

She was going to tell him about the rest; everything that her mother had said, that Wilson had come to see her and she had thrown him out, and that Anderson had come to see her. Then she thought better of it and decided that to keep the peace between the brothers, she should keep Anderson's interest in her quiet. She could just be friends with him, never letting Reed know that Anderson wanted her.

She thought of telling him all those things, but his kiss deepened and his arms grew tight around her, and then he picked her up and carried her up to his bedroom, standing her up beside his bed.

"I have not been able to stop thinking about you. You are all that is on my mind. You are taking over my heart, and all I want to do is have nothing between us but skin." He kissed her hungrily as he pulled her clothes away from her and she laughed and kissed him, peeling his clothes away as well, and before a few moments had passed, there was nothing between them but skin.

He laid her back in his bed and ran his hands over her dark body, caressing every curve. He let his fingers fondle every lovely part of her. She watched him gazing at her, kissing her, feeling what he had missed. It was as though she had stolen the very air from him and then after a long while, given it back and allowed him to breathe again. She felt her heart warming with love for this incredibly beautiful man.

He could not hold himself back from her for long, and soon his kisses on her body found their way to her mouth and she wrapped her legs around him and pulled him into her, filling herself with his need and finding rapture in their unity. They made love for a long while, clinging to each other, gasping, moaning in pleasure, touching, tasting, kissing and loving, moving with one another until they clung to each other in their orgasms, finding ecstasy together.

When they were laying in each other's arms afterward, Reed kissed her softly and then turned and opened the drawer of his nightstand, and he pulled out a box and opened it, revealing a stunning ring.

She gasped as he slid it on her finger and he kissed her again, brushing his lips against hers. "Marry me, Jillian. Marry me for love." Then he looked at her, his heart lodged in his throat and waited for her answer.

Jillian felt her heart swell with happiness and she laughed and said, "Yes!" then "Yes!" again, and she kissed him. Their closeness found them making love again minutes later, and they spent the better part of the day wrapped up in each other, kissing, holding and touching each other, bringing out every pleasurable sigh and moan of ecstasy.

When they surfaced for dinner, dressed and blissfully happy, Carter was extremely pleased to hear the news, and to see Jillian at their home.

"Jillian, I want you to move in with us here, tomorrow, if you are willing to," Reed said, and Carter agreed with him wholeheartedly. He looked as though he didn't want to take any chances on her getting away.

She thought about it for a moment and nodded, smiling at them both. "I would be glad to." She looked around and asked curiously, "Where is Anderson? We want to tell him the good news."

Carter shrugged his shoulder. "He said that he had some business to take care of. He was at a very important meeting this morning that needed more of his immediate attention and he said he'd be gone for a couple of days. I expect he will be back soon enough."

Jillian bit her lip in confusion, her thoughts tangled as she thought back to that morning. Anderson had been with her that morning. He had wanted to make love to her, he had begged her to be his wife and had come on to her as strong as any man ever had. Then, when she had turned him down, he had asked her to spend the whole day with him. She turned him down again.

How had he gone from wanting to spend the day with her to suddenly disappearing for an important meeting? She let the thoughts go, and focused on the two men who were in the room with her, in particular, the one who had put an engagement ring on her hand that afternoon.

143

Jillian was moved into the house the next day, and Carter provided moving services for her that accomplished the task in no time at all. Her mother was thrilled, Carter was beaming and had spent the afternoon with Kimiko in his office going over wedding details again, and by dinner, it was finished. Jillian saw while they were having their meal together that their families would make a good union, and that her mother might actually have chosen well for her. Carter was very welcoming and had told Jillian that their home was now hers and he fully expected her to make herself at home there.

She decided to take him up on it and the next day she was swimming in the enormous pool behind the house, playing in the water and basking in the sun when she heard her name and lifted her head from beneath the water to see Anderson kneeling beside the pool. He was grinning at her.

"Jillian!" he called out happily.

She swam to the stairs and walked out of the pool, water streaming down her hair and body, the sun glinting off her mahogany skin, and her jet black hair hanging in a curtain behind her. He whistled and walked to her with a grin and a towel.

"I don't want to cover you up because you are stunning enough to steal my breath away just looking at you, but I also don't want you to be cold," he said, wrapping the towel and his arms around her, then leaning down and kissing her lips slowly and sensually. His hands moved to cup her cheeks as he tasted her.

She gasped and pulled her face away from his, and he looked at her and cocked his head in curiosity. "What made you decide to come to me? What made you change your mind?" he asked, his hands on her back moved down over her hips and pulled her snugly to him, squeezing her hungrily.

Jillian shook her head and tried to take a step back from him. "Anderson, you don't understand. I'm not here for you," she said gently.

He blinked at her and his tight embrace loosened slightly. "What do you mean?"

She stepped back again and smiled a little at him. "Reed asked me to marry him and I said yes." She spoke quietly and tenderly, hoping that her words would hit him softer if her delivery was compassionate.

He stared at her for a moment and his composure was gone, his eyes filled with some strange panic, but then it was gone and he smiled at her and lifted her hands to his mouth, kissing her fingers. "If this is what you truly want, then I am pleased for you, of course, and I wish you every happiness. My brother is indeed a very lucky man to have a woman as special and precious as you to spend his life with."

She smiled back at him. "It is what I want, and I am happy. Thank you, Anderson."

He hugged her close and then let her go. "When will the special day be?"

"Our parents are planning it for a month from now." She smiled at him. "It's fast. I can't believe how fast it's happening. Reed and Carter have already had me move into the house here," she said, just a bit giddy.

He blinked in surprise. "You've moved in here? With Reed?" He stumbled over the words, watching her carefully.

Jillian nodded happily.

He looked like he was trying to swallow something that was too big for his throat.

"Are you staying in Reed's room or have they given you a room of your own?" he asked with obvious trepidation.

"Yes, I'm staying in Reed's room," she said quietly, seeing what he was getting at.

He took a deep breath and his smile faded. "Please don't think me rude or intrusive, but... have you... become intimate with Reed?"

She looked away from Anderson. "I really don't think that's your business," she said quietly. He lifted his hand and turned her face toward him.

"Please... Jillian. Trust in me. Please tell me." He looked deeply into her eyes. "You were untouched when we went to Las Vegas. You were pure... fresh, you were a virgin. Please tell me if that has changed; if Reed has taken that from you."

She looked up at him and said softly, "I gave myself to him, he didn't take anything from me at all."

Anderson looked away from her sharply, but not quite fast enough that she didn't notice the expression of anger and frustration that flickered across his face. He took a breath and looked back at her.

"Well, my girl, I've got some very important business to attend to. You come and see me anytime you need, for any reason. I'm always here for you." He leaned over to her and kissed her lips softly for a brief moment, and then smiled slightly, turned and walked away.

She watched him walk away for a moment, knowing that it must have been hard for him to hear her news, but confident that they would be able to remain friends. She was glad that she had him in her life; someone she could rely on and trust, a sort of friend within the family.

Needs separator

Reed walked into Anderson's office and sat at his desk. "What is it brother?" he asked.

Anderson smiled at him and offered him a scotch, which Reed accepted. "Thank you for coming in to talk with me," Anderson said as he handed the glass to Reed.

"I've come back from an important business meeting and discovered that you are engaged and Jillian is living here in the house. I suppose congratulations are in order," he said with a tight smile.

"Yes! It's really incredible that I've managed to pull it off, but somehow she likes me in spite of myself and she has agreed to marry me. I tell you, Anderson, she is the most incredible woman I've ever known. I can't believe I'm so lucky." Reed smiled at his brother.

Anderson leaned against his desk and looked down at his older brother. "I have to wonder, though, if you are really ready for this kind of commitment. I mean, there you were, living large and enjoying life, lovers left and right, nights out on the town, fast cars, sudden trips, fast and beautiful women... you had the life, Reed, and then father yanked the rug out from under you and told you that you were going to be married whether you liked it or not.

"You were pretty deep into Daisy when father told you that. I can't blame you, she is an extremely sexy woman. I can see your attraction to her. Is it really so easy for you to leave all of that behind and get married? Are you really sure this is what you want? Won't you miss the fun exciting days you have always lived? Won't you miss Daisy?"

Reed shook his head and smiled. "I'll tell you, I don't think anyone could be more surprised than me, Anderson, but the more I think about it, the more I want it. I wasn't really doing anything with my life, I was wasting it and I didn't realize it until I saw what I could have with Jillian. She's amazing. I want this more than anything in my life."

"You aren't going to miss screwing Daisy? As I understand it, she was pretty hot for you, and it was reciprocated much of the time." Anderson looked slyly at his brother.

"I don't miss her now. I guess I won't miss her in the future. I sent her on her way. I realized how much I was using her and I just couldn't keep doing that to her. She deserves better," Reed said with a guilty look.

"I take it then that you won't be seeing her as a lover on the side?" Anderson asked, looking at him carefully out of the corner of his eye.

"No," Reed answered. "I'm not interested in anyone but Jillian."

Anderson took a long drink of his scotch. "Well, it is a big change, are you sure you've really thought about it? I mean, staying true to one woman isn't exactly something you're good at. Your whole experience with women has been one of recycling them and not much caring about which one happened to be underneath you. This is a huge commitment for you.

"One woman? The rest of your life? Are you certain? I have to tell you, I didn't expect you to succeed at Carter's arranged marriage for you. I really thought you would buck at the idea of being tied to one woman and settling down. Have you really given it that much honest thought?"

Reed nodded with a grin. "I can't think of anything but her and the life we will have together."

Anderson swallowed the last of his scotch, set the glass on his desk, and then folded his arms in front of his chest. "What about the business? Father is going to hand you quite a bit of responsibility. You've never done anything to learn the business, you don't handle any part of it right now, and he's willing to put the reins right into your hands. Are you ready for that?"

Reed slumped slightly in his chair. "I am a little intimidated about that," he admitted. "I wish I had spent the time that you have on it, or even half the time you've spent. I would know a lot more. I'd be ready for it when Carter hands it over to me. You know what, though, I'll have you around, so I guess I will really rely on you to help guide me through it all and sort of be my right hand man." He smiled up at Anderson.

His brother clenched his teeth and returned a slightly forced smile. "Your right hand man. Do you realize that I've been working on this business since I was fourteen? Did you know it's been that long? You weren't around much at that point, after mom died and you discovered that no woman could resist you, you spent a lot of time out of the house and away from what father and I were doing here with the business. It's a huge responsibility, and even with my help, you would be lost running it."

Reed looked as though he were turning a little green. "I know I was gone quite a bit, but I'm willing to work at learning it. I want to lead the family I'm making like our father has. I'm sure with your help and dad's that it will continue to be a success. I'll always keep you on to help me. We can make it work together. You and me." His voice was hopeful and the happiness he felt about having Jillian there with him was lightening the heavy mood.

Anderson shook his head and looked out the window. "Your right hand man. Of course. That's my place." He walked over to the window and looked out of it. "Second in command. You'll have a beautiful bride and the inheritance, the house, the business and everything, and I can be your... right hand man." He slid his hands into his pockets and shook his head once more.

"Well, Reed. I suppose we ought to look at setting up an office for you, then. It would be helpful to have one here in the house. I'll have the builders draw up plans for you so we can make it official." He walked over to Reed. "If you are really sure that this is what you want to do."

149

Reed nodded. "It is. I have a responsibility, a duty to my family, and it's long overdue. Let's move forward with it, brother."

Anderson walked back around his desk and looked hard at Reed. "Yes. Responsibility and duty. You'll have plenty of that before you know it. More than you can imagine." He leaned back in his chair. "Well! I'd better get busy if I'm going to start arranging for you to take over the business…. Brother."

Reed stood up and set his empty glass on the desk. "I'm glad we talked. You've really helped me to put the future into focus. I appreciate it, Anderson. Thank you!" He left and Anderson picked up the phone as he was walking out the door.

Needs separator

Later that afternoon the bell at the front door rang and Reed answered it to see Daisy standing on the front steps. Her blonde curls were dancing in the breeze, tangling around her shoulders and her beautiful face. Her nearly sheer blouse was unbuttoned to the center of her melon-rounded breasts and her mini skirt barely covered her bottom. Her long bronzed legs stretched from the mini-hem down to red spike heels.

She rushed at Reed, wrapping her arms around him and kissing him immediately, her red lips opening his mouth as her arms clasped him tightly. She kissed him as if he was hers, hard and deep, before she let him go and grinned up at him.

"I gotta talk to you, baby," she said it in a loud hush.

He reached up and wiped her lipstick off his mouth. "Daisy, what are you doing here? You can't…" he began, but she hugged him again, pressing her body against his and looked up into his gorgeous face.

"Come on, Reed, this is important. I have to talk to you. In private. Right now. Come on, baby," she said in a low tone.

He sighed and looked around, and then walked her to one of the smaller downstairs sitting rooms for some privacy. He showed her into the room and closed the door behind them, then turned to look at her.

"What are you doing here? I told you that you needed to go start a new life! Daisy, I can't be with you anymore."

She grabbed his hand and walked him over to a sofa. "Come here, baby. We have to talk." She pulled him down beside her and then looked into his face. "Don't you miss me? Don't you miss all the fun we had?" She ran her hand up the inside of his thigh, but he pushed her hand away, wondering what on earth she was doing being there at all.

"Oh now, honey, don't be mean. I've missed you." She ran her fingers through his hair and pouted a little, turning to her side cuddling up close to him, pressing her breasts against the side of his chest. "You know, when you left me in Vegas like you did, I thought my heart was going to break right in half. You never want to talk about it, but you and I have feelings for each other, Reed, you love me. You want me. You always have, since that first night you saw me. Remember that night, Reed? When you came to the club and you were so hot for me that you just wouldn't take no for an answer, and you wound up waiting for me till I got off of work and then we went to that hotel and we played all night long? Remember? You and I played all... night... long..." she said seductively in his ear.

He remembered. He had never wanted another woman more and he had gotten her with hardly any effort, but then once he had her, he just couldn't quit. She was the closest thing to an almost regular lover that he had ever had. He hungered for her body like his body craved food. The memory both aroused and haunted him.

He felt horrible for the way that he had treated her, but there was not one memory with her which did not include amazing sex and his body was responding to her as she sat beside him on the sofa, so close, so warm, so ready. Always ready for him.

151

"I remember it." She whispered in his ear, kissing his neck softly. He pulled away slightly, but she reached her hand down between his legs and began to stroke him, and his traitorous body grew stiff beneath her hand. "Oh, baby, look at that. You remember, too."

He clamped his hand down on her wrist and pulled her hand away from him. "You can't be like that with me anymore, Daisy. What are you doing here?"

She stretched one long leg over his lap and before he could stop her, she was straddling him, and her arms were locked around his neck. She slid her body down close enough to his groin that her body was snug against his. "I'm not wearing any panties, Reed. You know I never wear panties when I'm with you," she whispered. "Come on, play with me.

Don't you want to anymore? I won't tell anyone. You can have anything you want, and I won't tell a soul. Come on. All you have to do is unzip these pants and I'll take care of everything else, just like I always do," she whispered hotly as she moved her body over the swell in his crotch and pressed her breasts near his face.

His hands grasped her waist and he pushed her away from him so that she was sitting on his knees. "Daisy, you have to stop. We cannot do this again, ever again. Now, answer me or I'm going to have to ask you to leave. What are you doing here?"

She leaned back over to him and whispered, her mouth inches from his, her eyes shining as she looked at him. "I just came to congratulate you, baby. You're going to be a daddy." Then she moved herself back down to his arousal and planted her bare crotch against it, and pressed her lips to his again, kissing him passionately as he sat there motionless and in shock.

Just then the door opened and Jillian walked in with Anderson right behind her.

Chapter 9

Reed heard the door and his eyes moved to the sound, though his body had seemed to stop functioning in response to the shock he was in. As if in slow motion, he saw Jillian and Anderson walk in, and Jillian's face fell in shock and horror, as Anderson looked at him with a smug smile.

He pushed Daisy off him and jumped up as quickly as he could. "This is not at all what it looks like!" he said, guilt flooding through him.

Daisy leaned around Reed's legs and ran her hand up his thigh, smiling at Jillian. Reed moved away from her quickly. Jillian stopped in her tracks and Anderson reached both his hands toward her, closing them on her hips and holding her back close to his chest as she gasped.

"What is going on in here?!" she asked, horrified.

"Jillian, it's nothing, truly, that's why I'm dressed. Daisy just showed up at the door and we came in here to talk. That's all. Then… uh… I guess she tried to kiss me, but nothing happened, and I didn't kiss her back." He was almost shouting in desperation.

Anderson leaned his head slightly over Jillian's shoulder. "We seem to have interrupted quite an intimate moment. What is it that you came to talk about, Daisy?" he asked in a calm tone.

She stood up and wrapped her hands around Reed's waist, then rubbed one hand on his chest. "I just came to congratulate Reed. You see, he and I are having a baby."

A pin could have been heard had it dropped anywhere in the room. The silence was deafening for a moment before Jillian turned to leave and found herself facing Anderson's chest. "I need to go," she whispered, but he held her tightly there and looked at Daisy.

"You're a stripper, Daisy. How do we know this is Reed's child?" Anderson asked in an accusatory voice.

Jillian looked over her shoulder at Daisy and Reed standing there looking at her. Daisy ran her hand over Reed's still solid erection beneath his pants and he grimaced and grabbed her hand away from him. "Reed is the only lover I've had for months and months. He's the only one I want, and every time we made love for at least the last month, he hasn't used protection. That's how nature works," she said, grinning up at him.

Jillian turned her head away and buried her face in Anderson's chest, trying her best to stem the torrent of tears that were flooding her eyes. She had believed him. She had trusted him, and now she was devastated by what he had done.

"Jillian!" Reed called out to her, but Daisy clamped onto his arm and Anderson leaned down to Jillian's ear and whispered, "Come with me." He walked her out of the room and they closed the door behind them.

Daisy pulled on Reed's arm and he turned and looked at her with anger and frustration. "What are you doing? What have you done?!" he gasped, trying to hold his emotions in check.

"Me?!" she asked in shock. "Reed, you did this to me. You did this to us. Now it's your responsibility to own up to your deeds and accept the consequences. You never used protection with me and now we have a baby on the way. A baby that we made in love. A baby that we created together. This is no more my fault than it is yours."

Reed knew that she was right. He sank down onto the sofa and buried his face in his hands. She curled up beside him and began to rub his shoulders. "I know it's hard. Believe me. I was alone when I found out, and I was so surprised, but baby, this is fate. This is fate telling us that we are supposed to be together."

She placed her hands on his face and turned it toward her. "Look at me, honey, it's you and me, and we're going to have a little tiny baby together. We're going to be a family! See the bright happy side of this. I love you. This is such a special time for us." She leaned over and kissed him again, moving her mouth over his, but he pulled away from her and stood up, walking to the windows and looking out.

"I can't believe this," he said quietly.

She rose and followed him. "Well, honey, you better believe it, because that's what's happening. You have a responsibility. You have a baby to look after now, and I'm not having a bastard kid. I want you to own up to your duty and marry me. You owe me that."

He turned around and stared at her. "I owe you no such thing! I don't have to marry you because you're pregnant!" he gasped.

She teared up and walked over to him. "Listen, baby. I love you. You know that. You've known that for a long time. Don't make me have this baby alone. Don't make me have a bastard child. Don't do that to your unborn baby. That's no way to start life. Is that what you really want? A bastard baby? This isn't quite what you had in mind, but you love me, you do.

"You just forgot for a little while because you were distracted with that woman that your dad wants you to marry, but you love me. You've loved me a long time, and now you have to step up to the plate. Marry me. Let's do this thing right and have this baby together. Come on. That's the right thing to do and you know it."

She looked up and him and wrapped her arms around his waist, hugging him and pressing her body up against him. "Reed, honey, we are going to have a baby!" She smiled happily at him and he thought he might throw up. Everything was suddenly upside down in his world. All of his plans, shot to hell. He had no idea what he was going to do.

All he knew was that he wanted to go to Jillian, but he didn't think he could. He had seen the look of shock and horror on her face, and it was more than he could honestly bear. He knew she was hurting horribly. She must be so confused; just as confused and sad as he was.

Daisy laid her head on Reed's chest. "Come on, Reed. Take care of me. You always said you would take care of me. Take care of me, and take care of your baby. Marry me," she said, looking up at him and lifting her mouth to his to kiss him again. He stood there in misery and turned his face from hers. "I don't want you like that, Daisy. Not anymore," he said quietly, and she began to weep and shake her head.

"Are you going to leave me like this? All alone? What are you going to do?" she asked.

He rubbed his hands over his face. "Well, for starters, I'm going to send you out to the pool house. You can stay there until we figure out what's going on. I'll have the staff stock the house for you. Give me some time and I will come out in a while and talk with you. We'll figure it out." He pulled her into a hug and then walked her out to the pool house, settled her in and left her there.

Needs separator

Anderson took a weeping and distraught Jillian to his office where he closed the door and locked it behind him. He walked her over to the sofa that was near the windows and sat her down on it, holding her close to him.

"I'm so sorry this has happened." He spoke quietly to her. "I had a bad feeling something like this might come up, and I hoped that it wouldn't, but here it is, and there's not much that we can do about this. My God, sweet girl, I'm so sorry." He held her close to his chest and stroked her hair and her cheek as she cried on him. Then he leaned over and kissed the top of her head

"How could this happen?" she asked in vain. "What's going to happen now? He can't marry me if he has a child with her!" She wept harder and Anderson continued to pet her and then he leaned down and softly kissed her forehead and stroked her neck.

"He's a selfish womanizing man who is only interested in himself and a good time. He's not concerned with you, otherwise he wouldn't have been there on the couch with her, kissing her and making out with her. Then for her to announce like that that they are having a child... how awful for you. What a heartache. I'm so sorry you have to go through this!

"You don't deserve it at all. You're such a sweet, beautiful, kind, loving woman. You deserve someone who treats you with love and respect, someone you can trust who will always be there for you and never hurt you," he intoned quietly into her ear while she cried. He wiped away her tears and kissed her cheek slowly and gently, rocking her in his arms.

"How could it happen? What on earth am I going to do now?" she whispered through her tears. "I was going to marry him! I wanted a family with him! I thought we were going to spend the rest of our lives together and now I just have no idea what to do!"

"We'll figure it out together, my girl, you and me. You aren't alone. I'm here with you. I'm here for you," he whispered, kissing her cheek again and wiping her tears away. "You'll make it through this with me by your side. You aren't alone. I've got you, my girl, I've got you. Come here. Come let it all out." He stroked her hair, running his hands through it, caressing it and wiping the tears from her cheeks.

"I'm here for you, Jillian, my Jillian, I will always be here for you," he spoke in the barest whisper, then tilted her brokenhearted face up to his and kissed her cheek, kissed each tear away, and she closed her eyes as he did. Then his mouth moved slowly and softly to her lips, kissing them gently, sweetly, as she wept, and before she realized it, she was kissing him back for a moment, tasting her own tears on his lips, and he held her tightly to him, but then she turned away and shook her head.

"I can't. Anderson, we can't be like that with each other. You are supposed to be my brother and my friend," she said miserably. "I want Reed, but I'm so confused! What am I going to do now?"

He reached his hand up and stroked her hair and her face. "I know, my girl, I know. It's all so difficult. I didn't mean to add to your confusion. You know I will be here for you in any way that you need me. It's just that I have such strong feelings for you and I hate to see you so hurt, so devastated by my brother, yet again.

"You deserve so much more. You deserve a man who will love you and take care of you, not break your heart every time you turn around. I know you are intent on being with my brother right now, but if he should choose to be with Daisy and raise their child together, then please consider me as an alternative. Please consider marrying me.

"I won't ever let you down. I'm here for you, and you can count on me. Trust in that. Remember that." He kissed her mouth again; a gentle and tender kiss that felt like an anchor in the storm to her, again. She looked at him in uncertainty, wondering if perhaps he might be right.

"I'll think about it," she said quietly.

"That's all I ask," he whispered, stroking her hair again.

She wiped the tears from her face and placed her hands on her knees. "Now what do I do?" she asked in a misty cloud of doubt.

He took her hands and pulled her up to her feet. "I know just the answer to that. Come with me." He led her to the door of his office and opened it, and then walked her upstairs. He took her to a different area of the upstairs that she hadn't been to before, and she looked around in amazement at the dark opulent wood and rich elegance of the house.

He opened a door and ushered her into a bedroom that was one of the most beautiful she had ever seen. There was a massive mahogany canopy bed footed with a chaise lounge, and adjacent to the chaise was an enormous fireplace. There were floor to ceiling windows that overlooked a garden and he showed her a private bathroom in marble and glass. There was a walk-in closet and a balcony off of the main area in the bedroom.

She looked all round her in amazement. He placed his hands upon her shoulders and then lifted her chin to look at him. "I want you to move your things into this room. I know you are staying in Reed's room, and that was alright until his situation changed this morning. You need your own space, your own privacy and somewhere that you can think and relax. A sanctuary, of sorts. This will be your room until you decide what is best for you. Let me give you this, at least," he said, touching her cheek.

Jillian nodded and turned away from him, looking around herself at the breathtaking room. It was then that she saw a door she hadn't seen before, and she walked over to it.

"What is this? Another closet?" she asked, turning the handle and opening it. It opened into another bedroom, and she walked in and realized that it was a room that was inhabited regularly.

Anderson walked in behind her with a smile on his face and placed his hands on her hips, speaking quietly over her shoulder."This is my room. I'll leave the door between our rooms closed, of course, but always unlocked, and if you ever want to come into this room for any reason, you are most welcome to. I would be glad for your company any time you wish to share it with me."
She felt nerves in her stomach tighten and she turned toward him. "Anderson, I'm really not sure what's going to happen."

"I know. Please don't feel awkward, it's just happens that this particular guest room adjoins mine. It's going to be fine. I won't open that door unless you want me to. You are safe and you will be in a place where you can have some privacy and some space to think about what you will do. I'll have the staff move your belongings into your new room right away. Please," he said, leading her back into her room, "make yourself comfortable."

She might not have been sure about what she was going to do about Reed and Anderson, but she did know she needed the space and privacy that Anderson was offering. She had a lot to work through and think about, so she allowed the move, and in no time at all, her belongings had been moved into the new bedroom.

Reed took Daisy out to the pool house and settled her into the room there. It was a two bedroom, two-bath facility with a kitchen, a deck, and a living room area. It was the same place that Jillian had discovered the two of them having intercourse the day that Reed asked Jillian to marry him. When he thought about it, it made him sick. It was not what he wanted now, and he felt enormous shame over his past actions and was remorseful that they were affecting his current life choices.

Daisy didn't have much with her, and the staff was able to fully stock the place quickly for her.

"Now, this is not a permanent move for you," Reed told her as they stood in the living room. "This is only a place for you to stay for now, until we figure out what's going to happen with you and…" his tongue tripped over the words, "…and the baby."

She walked up to him and wrapped her arms around him. "That should be easy to figure out, Reed. You're my lover. We're having a baby. You should marry me and love me for the rest of my life."

He pushed her arms away from him. "No, Daisy, it isn't that easy. You and I were never more than a fling and I was foolish and didn't use protection with you. I was irresponsible. Now I have consequences I have to face and a fiancé who I have to try to work this out with."

Daisy glared up at him. "You can't still be thinking of marrying her! I'm pregnant! How can you even consider marrying another woman? Reed, I am carrying your child!"

He shook his head at her. "I'm planning on it because I love her. That's what we were going to do. It's what our families want us to do. You were never supposed to be in the picture. I was never supposed to have a child. I don't know what's going to happen, I haven't talked to her about this yet. Look, just stay here and make yourself comfortable. Let me know if you need anything."

She locked her arms around him and pressed her body up against his. "I need you, Reed. I need you to love me and stay with me. The baby needs you."

Reed sighed and pushed her away, then shoved his hands into his pockets. "I need some time to digest the news you've given me, and I need you to remember that right now, I am engaged to another woman, a woman I love very much and who I want to spend the rest of my life with.

"Please don't act like you have been acting since you walked in the door here, we are not lovers any longer, and you can't touch me like you have been. You and I saw the end of our relationship when I left you in Las Vegas. I made it clear that you and I were finished then. I am committed to her, I am hers now, and you need to respect that. At the very least until we have our situations all figured out. Please, at least extend me the courtesy of some respect," he said kindly but firmly.

She pouted in dejection, but she nodded and plopped down on the sofa, grabbing a pillow and holding it to her. "Alright, but you need to really think about what you're doing."

He left her and went to his father's office. Carter was on the phone when Reed walked in. He smiled at his son, closed his conversation and hung up the phone.

"How are you doing, son?" he asked with a jovial smile. "You won't believe it. Your wedding is already making headlines in the business world and Jillian's uncles will be here for the ceremony. They've agreed to an extended stay so that we can discuss merging the companies and expanding here in the states.

"They have technology that you would never believe, son, and your marriage is the key to making that part of our family business. I'm so pleased with you for finally getting it together. Well done, my son," he said with a smile.

Reed sat down slowly and awkwardly. "Well, Carter, that's good to hear. There has been a development this morning that we need to talk about."

Carter tilted his head and rested his hands in his lap. "Oh? And what would that be?"
His tone was friendly, but his eyes were focused sharply on his son.

Reed rubbed his fingers over his forehead and decided that the best thing to do would be just to come out and say it. "Well, I was seeing a girl named Daisy, off and on for a little while right before Jillian came into the picture, and Daisy came to visit me this morning. She said she had some news for me. For us. Uh… she said she's pregnant. I put her in the pool house as a guest until we could sort out what we are going to do about it."

Carter glared at his son with steely eyes. "We aren't going to do anything about it. You are engaged and you are getting married. If this girl Daisy is pregnant, then it's her problem. If I was you, I would take her down to a clinic this morning and have that problem taken care of. Get rid of that baby, Reed, you are just about to make the biggest change in your life and you don't need some irresponsible accident like this wrecking your future!"

He leaned forward in his chair and continued, as the level of his voice began to rise. "I thought you said you loved Jillian, that you two were actually going to be married because you wanted to spend your lives together, and now look at you! You're about to let a mistake from your past screw up your entire future! To be honest, I can't believe this hasn't come up before now, the way you get around with so many women.

"There's a lot more riding on this than just your future, Reed. You are about to be handed the reins to our family fortune, our company, and everything we have. I am not going to hand all of that to a fool who can't even figure out how to have an affair without getting a woman pregnant!"

Carter rose up and walked around his desk, all the while keeping his eyes on Reed. "Don't you dare mess up this business deal for me. This is non-negotiable, son. *Non-negotiable.* You will marry Jillian. You will bring our families together and we will close this deal with them. I am not about to lose a fortune or jeopardize the future of this family over your indecencies!

"You get that woman out of my pool house, you take her downtown and you get your little mistake taken care of immediately!"

Reed felt like he was going to vomit. He hadn't quite been sure what his father would say, but the reaction he was getting wasn't what he had expected at all.

"Does Jillian know about this?" Carter asked, his anger beginning to seethe.

Reed nodded. "Yes, she knows."

"What did she say?" Carter asked worriedly.

"She left with Anderson. I'm not sure where she is yet. I was busy getting Daisy out to the pool house and then I came to see you to find out what you wanted me to do about this. I'm sure she's pretty upset." Reed sighed, knowing he was going to have a hell of a time explaining any of it to her. He wanted her to stay with him; he wanted to marry her and make her his wife, but now there was a baby to think of.

Now there was a child in the picture. His child, growing inside of Daisy, and he could not have been more conflicted about what to do.

His father scoffed. "Perhaps I should have arranged for her to marry Anderson instead. He's always put the family and the business first. I gave you the chance because you are my firstborn, the oldest, the heir to the kingdom, as it were, and you have done nothing but give me reason after reason to hand it to your younger brother.

"I'm about out of patience with you, Reed. You either get rid of that mistake and the girl in the pool house and marry Jillian, or you are out of here. No money, no inheritance, nothing at all. I want a decision made on this immediately. I'm right in the middle of your wedding plans and the last thing I need is for you to screw that up for yourself, your bride, our family and our business." Carter returned to his seat and narrowed his eyes at his son. "Go take care of it, now."

Reed stood up and pushed his hands into his pockets. "Thanks for the talk, Carter." Then he walked out and carried the weight of the world on his shoulders with him. He thought he would make one more stop and he poked his head into Anderson's office. His brother was sitting at his desk working, as usual.

"Busy, Anderson?" he asked casually.

Anderson waved him in and Reed walked in and closed the door. His brother turned and looked at him, a half-smile on his face.

"Well, if it isn't the new father to be. How are you, Reed?" Anderson stood up and poured them both a drink.

"I'm a wreck. I have no idea where Jillian is or how she's doing, Daisy is set up in the pool house as a guest and she's pregnant with my child. Carter just told me that I have to take Daisy downtown to a clinic and have the 'mistake taken care of' or I will be disinherited and kicked out of the family and the house. I'm not doing very well."

Anderson smiled to himself and handed Reed his scotch. "Well, that's a lot on one plate, Reed. Jillian is fine, I took care of her. What are your thoughts on the matter? Surely you aren't going to listen to father on this."

"I don't know what to do. I thought I'd come and talk with you about it before I speak with Jillian. She'll want to know what I'm going to do and I honestly don't know right now. I have no answer for her. What do you think, Anderson? What would you do?" Reed looked up at his brother for some kind of answer and direction.

Anderson sat down beside Reed and looked at him earnestly. "I would keep the child. Think of it! Reed, you have created a new life! You're going to be a father! There's a little person inside of Daisy right now that is there, living and growing, because of you!

"You have an obligation now, Reed. You have a duty and a responsibility to that child to care for it and bring it into this world. You have a duty to it to raise it and care for it, to teach it and help it grow up. Be a father, Reed. Be a dad. That's your child out there inside that beautiful woman. I can't even believe you would consider killing it, not even for a moment!"

Reed took a long pull of his drink and rubbed his hand over his face. "I've thought about that. Carter made the point that if I keep this child, then I'll be jeopardizing everything he has worked for to build up this family, and that I will be costing the family an unimaginable future. It's an enormous responsibility. I have far more than just myself to think of here. I have to consider Jillian and Daisy, you, Carter, and now a baby in the mix. I have no idea what would be best to do here."

Anderson took a different tack. "Reed, I'm just going to come out and say this. It's time to pay the piper. You have led a wild and reckless life and now it has caught up with you. You have no business trying to get out of this. You have a duty and responsibility to that woman out there and to your unborn child, and everything else comes second.
Everything else.

"You want to know what to do? You pack up and leave with Daisy, you help her through her pregnancy, and then you stay with her through the delivery and you help her raise that baby of yours. That's what you do. There is no other option. There is no alternative. You screwed around, this is the consequence, and you have to own up to it. You have to face it.

"You had several chances to take your place in this family and you screwed them up left and right. You always have. Well, now you've gone and made your own family, and since you have never acted with any responsibility or respect toward this family, you owe it doubly to the family that you just created to give them your all, for the rest of your life. That's what you do. It's what you have an obligation to do." Anderson sat back in his chair and swallowed his scotch.

Reed buried his face in his hands and moaned. "What about Jillian?"

"If you really wanted her, you would have been thinking of her the whole time, and this wouldn't have happened, but you weren't. It's too late, Reed. You've lost her. Your actions and mistakes have taken you down another path. You're going to have to let her go and focus on what is really important now, and that is the baby that needs you more than anyone else in this family, including Jillian.

"She didn't want you to begin with. You two were forced into the marriage. Just let her go. You're still at the beginning with her, so you aren't really walking out on her or hurting her much. Let her go and take up the yoke of duty that you owe to that child you made."

Reed sighed and nodded. "Couldn't I marry Jillian and just support Daisy and the baby financially?"

"What kind of a father is that? Do you want that child to be born a bastard? Is that how you want your child to be seen by the world? As a mistake? As unwanted errors not even worthy of your name? Marry Daisy and give your heir a proper life, Reed, a home, a family, your name. Give that child of yours some honor. Don't wait

167

on this. You own up to your actions, marry Daisy and make it right. This shouldn't even be a question in your mind. Where are your values and morals? You were raised better than that."

Anderson took another long pull from his glass and watched his brother carefully.

"How am I going to support a family? If I choose Daisy and the baby, Carter is going to cut off every penny to me!" Reed was dizzy at the thought of how he could handle the responsibility without the income.

"We have countless contacts in this area. I'm sure I could help you get a job somewhere. You know I can't do anything to help you from our end here with the family business, it's all written up that way, but I can certainly help you find some position with one of our associates or even one of our competitors. They'd love to get their hands on you, I'd be willing to bet. It would be so easy. You go, you marry Daisy, you get a job and a nice place, you raise your child and take care of your family. That's what you do."

Reed thought carefully about it. Anderson's answers were far closer to his own ideals than Carter's were, but the thought of losing Jillian was almost more than he could stand.

"But, Jillian…" he said quietly.

"She's a casualty in your wild and chaotic lifestyle, Reed, and that's just the way that it has got to be. You made your bed, now you have to lay in it and take care of your obligations. Jillian is a sweet dream that is no longer yours. Let her go. You owe this to Daisy and your baby." Anderson seemed adamant.

Reed knew he was probably right. There was no other way around it, really. He did have an obligation; a situation that he created, albeit unknowingly, and he was going to have a very high price to pay for it. The price of a lifetime of happiness with Jillian.

The Final Chapter

Jillian was sitting in her new room when there was a knock at the door. She answered it, pulling the door open and saw Reed standing there. He looked wrung out. She opened the door all the way and asked him into the room.

"So you moved into a new bedroom," he said rather glumly.

"I just needed some space and some privacy so I could think. That's all. I didn't know what was going on with you and… everything," she replied, folding her arms across her chest.

He walked to the chaise at the foot of her bed and sat down. "Well, I've really made a mess of things this time. I can't even believe it myself, now."

She walked over to him and sat beside him. "So what's going to happen?" she asked, not really wanting to know.

Reed shrugged. "I guess that part of that is up to you. Carter wants me to take Daisy to a clinic downtown and have the 'mistake taken care of'. Anderson wants me to own up to my responsibility and take care of the child, as any good father should. Daisy wants me to marry her and help her raise the baby."

"What do you want?" Jillian asked him, wishing she had the courage to look up into his eyes, but finding that she did not.

He didn't hesitate at all. "I just want you," he answered. "I want to marry you and spend the rest of my life with you. I love you. You are all that I want. Unfortunately, it's just not that easy now. I made some big mistakes and I wasn't careful when I was with Daisy, and now I am not the only one who will have to pay the price.

"Carter said he's going to disinherit me and kick me out of the house if I don't get rid of the pregnancy and Daisy. He's bent on going forward with our marriage and the business dealings with your uncles. Hell bent. Anderson is in the completely opposite camp. He's adamant that I face up to what I've done and meet my obligations."

Reed stood up and walked to the fireplace, his back to Jillian. He pushed his hands down into his pockets for the umpteenth time that morning. "What do you think?" he asked quietly.

Jillian spoke softly. "I knew you would ask me that, and I'm sorry to say that I have no answer for you. This is your choice. It's your responsibility. It's your life, it's your child, and it is your decision to make. I can only wait for whatever you decide to do, I guess. I'm not going to try to persuade you in any direction, because I don't want your choice to be influenced by me at all. Whatever you choose to do has to come from your own heart, and not from anyone else."

He turned and walked toward her. "If I could choose you and it wouldn't hurt anyone else, I would choose you," he said in a whisper. She rose up and hugged him.

"I know that. I'm so sorry that this is happening, but you do have some very important decisions to make, and no one else can do that for you," she said.
He held her for a long time, and they didn't speak; they only stood with each other, their arms around one another, their hearts aching for a viable option, but in the end there was no easy answer, and Reed kissed her softly and walked out of the door.

Jillian laid on her bed and cried until she fell asleep, and when she woke up, there was only one person she wanted to talk to. She called her father.

He was still in Japan working with her uncles, but he had told her that he would be home soon, and then they could spend some time together. She missed him terribly. There was no one in the world that she connected with the way that she did with her father. They had the truest, strongest bond of anyone in her life, and in the midst of the turmoil she found herself in now, and she only wanted to speak to him.

Samson answered quickly and she cried when she heard his voice.

"What is it, baby girl?" he asked in a concerned tone.

"Daddy, things are such a mess here." She sighed through her tears. "Reed found out this morning that his ex-girlfriend is pregnant. She came here to the house. She wants him to marry her and raise their baby together."

"Oh, no," her father said, and his warm sympathy reached through the phone to her. "I'm so sorry to hear that, baby. How are you handling it?"

"I have no idea what to do. I'm so confused and hurt. I'm so sad about it. Reed and I are falling in love. We actually want to be together and we agreed to get married because we wanted to, not because Carter and Mother told us we had to. Now this has happened and I don't know what to do!" She wept as she explained it all to him.

"What has he decided to do?" Samson asked quietly.

"He doesn't know what he's going to do. He said he wants to be with me, but he feels like he has a responsibility to her and the baby. He's torn," she said in a thin voice.

"Well, he certainly does have that," Samson said. "No matter what he chooses, whether it is to stay with you or to be with her, that baby isn't going anywhere, so have you thought about whether or not you would be willing to become a step-mother to a newborn baby? Because that's just what will happen if you stay with him and get married. You'll have to deal with the fact that he has a family with her as well as with you, and you will have to share him with her in a paternal way, for the rest of your life."

Jillian hadn't thought about that. "Oh Daddy, I didn't even think that far ahead. That's not everything, either. Reed's brother Anderson has been after me. He wants me to marry him and not his brother. He says he has feelings for me and that if I marry him, our families will still be able to be together."

Samson chuckled a little. "My goodness! I left for just a little while and look at all the chaos that got stirred up. Well, how do you feel about Anderson?"

"I think of him as a friend. He's really nice to me. He's always looking out for me, but he's also always trying to get me to choose him, too. He's really been there for me through everything with Reed. I feel like I can trust him and count on him, but that's about it. I don't have any romantic feelings for him. At least, not like he has for me. I just really want Reed," she answered.

Her father sighed. "Well, baby girl, if you don't have feelings for Anderson, then keep it a friendship. As far as Reed goes, it sounds like you would be taking on an awful lot if you and Reed stayed together, so I think you need to really give it some consideration. Are you willing to share your life with their child and raise that child like it's your own for the rest of your life?

"Even if Daisy keeps the child, it will still be around you sometimes, and you will be a step-mother. Think carefully about that and be sure that it's a commitment you are ready to make. The other thing is, you know you don't have to marry either of them. I realize that your mother is pushing you hard to marry Reed for the business dealings, but those can probably be made without your marriage, if both sides want them bad enough. All I want for you is to know that you are happy. That's my priority."

"Thank you, Daddy. You've really given me a lot to think about," she said, giving him a farewell and finally hanging up. She spent a good deal of time considering everything and came to a conclusion. She texted Reed and asked him to come to her room, and minutes later, he was there at the door looking extremely anxious.

"What is it?" he asked, not sure if he could take anymore.

"I've made a decision about what I'm going to do." By the look on her face, he was certain that he wasn't going to like it.

"What is it?" he asked, his heart in his throat.

"I can't stand to see you torn up like this, not knowing what to do, feeling like you have obligations in every direction, and seeing you torn by all of it, so I'm going to give you your freedom. I'm going to go back to my parents' house and then you won't have to choose between your child and me." She reached for his hand and opened it, palm up, then placed her engagement ring inside his hand.

"I love you, Reed, and I want to spend the rest of my life with you. I can't stand between you and your child and I don't know if I'm ready to be a step-mother to a newborn baby. Especially to a baby you are having with Daisy. I feel like it would be selfish of me to stay here and if I leave, then it frees you up to make the best choices for your child, and I think that your child should come first." She sighed. "I'm so sorry."

Reed knew he wasn't going to like what she had to say. His hand closed around the ring in his palm and he closed his eyes and pulled Jillian to him, holding her tightly against his chest as tears began to fall from his eyes.

He wept and she wept with him as they let go of what they had both learned to want together. After a long time, he looked down at her and lowered his face to hers, kissing her gently, and looking sadly into her eyes.

"You will always be the one I wanted more than anyone else in the world. You will always have my heart. I love you, Jillian," he whispered to her.

"And you for me as well," she said back to him.

He made his exit quietly and she watched him go, then she packed up her things and left instructions to have it all taken back to her parent's house, and she dressed to leave. She had come to think of this house as the home that she would probably be in for the rest of her life, but now it was just a place she was leaving.

She had no idea what the rest of her life was going to be like, now that she would not have Reed in it, or any man for that matter, at least for a while.

She thought about what Anderson had become to her. He'd been such a good friend, such a wonderful supporter for her. She felt that she owed it to him to say goodbye and she smiled, thinking about the door between their rooms. He had said that it would be closed but never locked so that she knew she was always welcome to come into it. She thought that she would see if he was in his room for her to say goodbye to him, and she quietly turned the handle and opened the door, walking in just a few steps before she heard him and it was then that she heard a woman as well and she stopped in her tracks. The sound of the woman was completely unexpected and it caught her totally off guard.

Her eyes flew to the bed and she gasped silently at what she saw there. Daisy was bent over the side of Anderson's bed and she was nude. He was standing behind her, his pants dropped down to his ankles and his body planted deeply inside of her, as he pumped away at her, his hands reaching around to the front of her, clenched to her full round breasts.

The sight of them having intercourse was not all that stopped Jillian in her tracks. Their conversation froze her in place.

"You'd better get pregnant this time, Daisy. We are running out of time to make this plan work! I can't keep screwing you like this day in and day out, trying to fill in for what my brother didn't do." Anderson almost growled at her as he shoved himself into her over and over.

"I haven't been able to get Reed to sleep with me. Not since Vegas," she said, almost apologetically.

Jillian could not believe her eyes. No matter what, Reed had to know what was going on. She slipped her phone from her pocket and silently texted him, telling him to come back to her room quietly and not to say anything when he got there.

Anderson moaned loudly as he worked away at Daisy, grinding himself into her, and finally he climaxed and his orgasm was delivered deeply into her. He grunted in pleasure, and then let go of her body, pulled himself from the depths of her, and then yanked his pants back up and buckled them.

"Listen, Daisy, we've got to make this plan work fast, or it isn't going to work. If the last time Reed screwed you was in Vegas, then you don't have much time to get pregnant before it becomes obvious that it isn't his baby you are carrying. You can't screw this up for me. We have one shot to get it right. I get you pregnant, you make Reed marry you and you two leave.

"I will give you the million dollars I agreed to, and you two can live together, in love, high off the hog for a long time, and have your little family. I will inherit the business that is rightfully mine, I get the house and everything, and I get Jillian. My father gets his business deal with her Japanese family and I become the hero that made it happen. I become the golden boy. Everyone wins."

By that time, Reed was standing behind Jillian and listening to every word his brother was saying. He texted his father and told him to get to Anderson's room immediately.

"I've had to play second fiddle to him all of our lives, and that is about to change. You two run off together with your little family, I take care of the family here, and it all works out. Happy endings for all of us. Reed will never know it's not his kid you had. After all, it will still be family. Biologically, the kid would be his niece or nephew, and then after that kid you two can have your own together.

"We've just got to get you pregnant to get the whole thing started, and we've got to get you pregnant fast." Anderson smacked her on the ass as she worked herself back into her mini skirt. "I will say that

I don't mind doing the dirty work, though. You are one hot woman."
He smirked at her.

Jillian had heard all she could stand to hear. She marched into the room where Anderson could see her and she fumed at him. "How dare you! What do you think you're doing! You are wrecking lives!"

Anderson looked at her in shock and reached for her. "What are you doing here?" he asked in a panic.

She backed away from him and glared at him angrily. "Don't you touch me! You told me I could come into your bedroom any time at all, and I did, only to find you having sex with Daisy! You're trying to get her pregnant and make Reed believe that it is his child?! That's the most despicable thing I've ever heard of! How could you do that to your own brother?"

Carter had just opened the door at that point and he looked from the half-naked Daisy to Anderson, and then from Jillian to Reed, who had come into full view from Jillian's room.

"What in the hell is going on in here! I demand answers right now!"

Jillian put her hands on her hips and narrowed her eyes at Daisy and Anderson. "I saw these two having sex and Anderson was telling her he needed to get her pregnant so that Reed would think it was his baby, and then she could get him to marry her and leave with her. Anderson said he would give Daisy a million dollars for doing it. Then he said he was going to marry me and that he would unite my family with yours so he could inherit everything and have it all."

Reed's jaw fell open and he stared at Anderson. "What do you mean you were going to marry Jillian? You're my brother! She is my fiancée!"

Jillian spoke over her shoulder to Reed. "He's been coming on to me constantly since Vegas. He tried to get me to sleep with him on the plane on the way back, and that's when he started asking me to marry him instead of you. He kept telling me not to marry you, telling me that I deserved someone who really loved me, who really wanted me and who wouldn't hurt me, and here he is lying, cheating and deceiving his own family right under all your noses. Here he is, sleeping with your ex, trying to get her pregnant."

Reed launched himself at Anderson and landed a right hook on the side of his brother's face that laid him out flat on the floor. "How dare you go after either one of these women! How dare you try to pull such a low down shady trick on your own family! You are no brother of mine! I trusted you! How could you do this?"

Carter stepped in and pushed Reed away from Anderson. "How dare you meddle with what you know damn well to be the most important business transaction of my entire career! I had a plan! Marry my oldest son and heir to Jillian, and we move forward from there! At no time were you supposed to be a backup to that plan! You could easily have destroyed the whole thing for all of us!"

Carter glared at Daisy. "You! Are you pregnant with Reed's baby?"

She began to cry miserably. "No…" she sobbed.

"What the hell were you doing in here with Anderson?" Carter demanded.

She cried, looking at Reed for help and seeing that she would get none from him. She decided to come clean. "Anderson came to me and asked me to go with Reed to Vegas so that he could bring Jillian down and show her that Reed was with me.

"We did it, and she saw us. Actually, she has walked in on us a couple of times, but Anderson said that would make her leave Reed and then I could have him and Anderson could have Jillian, but it didn't work, so he came to me again and said he had another plan.

"He said Jillian had just moved into the house here and that the only way we were going to split them up now was if I told Reed I was pregnant. The only problem is that I wasn't pregnant, so Anderson said he'd get me pregnant and it would all be in the family, then

Reed would think it was his baby and he would marry me. Anderson said he'd probably be kicked out of the family, but it would be okay because he was going to give me a million dollars to do it.

"Then I would have Reed all to myself and we could have a family and Anderson would get Jillian and all the money and the house and the business." She was sobbing by the time she got to the end of it, and Carter was furious.

"Young woman, get your clothes on, get your belongings and take yourself from this house. I never want to see your face here again," he hollered at her.

Reed pulled Jillian into his arms and held her. She was shaking, she was so angry, and tears were spilling down her cheeks. Anderson had pulled himself up off the floor and was holding back some considerable rage.

"*This*! This is the thanks I get for working all of my life to build up your business, father, and Reed gets to live a life of wild abandon, screwing all the women he wants and leaving a path of destruction and chaos in his wake. I have to keep going after him to clean up all his legal messes, and then you choose him above me to marry the virgin bride and unite the families in the biggest deal of our lives!

"After everything I've done for you! After all of the years I have given you, the sacrifices I have made, and the progress I've brought to the company! This is the thanks I get!" He was yelling at the top of his lungs, looking from one to the other of all of them. "I'm always second to him! Always! Second born, second best, last chosen!"

Carter was fuming as well. "Your insecurity and selfishness almost cost this family the biggest deal of our lives! What in the hell were you thinking?" he demanded.

"I was thinking I would finally, just once, get what's coming to me, but I got left out again!" he yelled at his father.

Carter stepped toward him and spoke coldly. "You are going to get what is coming to you. You will pack up every belonging that you have and you will leave this house. I do not expect to ever see you again because you have no reason to come back here. You may take with you one tenth of your original inheritance. That inheritance was never in question. It was never going to be part of what your brother was getting.

"I had other plans for you that would have rewarded you for all that you have contributed. I am not blind. I have seen all that you have done, but you are impatient and you would not wait until the time was right, you wanted what you thought you deserved, what you thought was rightfully yours, before it was time to have it.

"Now you will get just exactly what you deserve, and it is quite a bit less than what you would have gotten. You will take that one tenth and you will never darken my doorstep again. Do you understand me?"

Anderson shivered and kept his eyes on his father. "I do. I'll be gone by tomorrow."

"Good-bye," Carter said, and then turned to Reed and Jillian. "I expect that you two will continue with your plans as they were before your brother intervened?"

Reed spoke up for both of them immediately. "Yes. We will, just as we planned."

Carter nodded. "Very good. I will go and talk with Kimiko then, and we will move forward with the wedding plans." He walked out of the bedroom and closed the door behind him. Anderson turned and looked at them both. His teeth were gritted in anger and his eyes glistened with tears of rage.

Reed shook his head and led Jillian from the room, walking back through the door into her room, and closing and locking the door behind them. He held her closely to him while she cried, and he wept with her. He had almost lost her, and he had in fact lost his brother.

A man whom he had believed to be one of his only allies; someone he could trust and rely upon, a man he admired and respected, and who had let them all down because of his greed and his egotistical insecurities.

"Will you move back into my room with me?" Reed asked with a sad smile.

She nodded. They walked together to his room, to their room, and he curled up with her in their bed and held her while they talked a little about what had happened, and then left the talking for later. They found solace in each other's arms, making love through the afternoon, replenishing their joy in each other. As Reed was moving inside of Jillian, making her moan with unbridled pleasure, he told her softly, "You are the only woman I ever want in my life, in my bed, in my arms. Just you, Jillian, always." And she knew he was telling her the truth.

All of her doubts were gone. All of the pain and confusion, the anger and misunderstandings vanished, and in their place was deep, real, true love that would last them the rest of their lives.

Weeks later, she was dressed in a gown of white that cascaded from her lovely figure down to the floor. Her father was in a traditional kimono, as were the rest of her family who had come for the ceremony. Her mother was beyond pleased, gliding around like a geisha, entertaining the guests and family members, and Carter was hooked at the elbow to her uncles who had flown in from Japan for her wedding, and for the business that would be undertaken afterward.

The ceremony was simply beautiful, held in the grand and lush gardens behind the house. Everything around the ceremony was decked out in flowers and draped material, an orchestra played, and doves were released after their vows were spoken.

Both Reed and Jillian felt the absence of his brother, Anderson, but neither one of them felt that he should be there. Nothing was said about him by anyone during or after the ceremony, and at the reception, their joy was only increased as Jillian's uncles presented them with the gift of a long touring honeymoon.

The day ended in a glorious sunset and as the moon rose, Jillian and Reed were nestled into the cozy bed at the back of their private jet.

As they flew away into the night and into the rest of their lives, Jillian thought about all the things that brought them to where they were that night.

"It's so strange to think that even after everything that happened, it still wound up this way, that we are together and that we want to be with each other. I'm glad we did it. I know at first the idea of an arranged marriage made me so angry, and all I wanted to do was leave you and never have to see you again, but our parents were wise in putting us together. You are all I could ever wish for and want." She smiled at him and kissed him sweetly.

"Well, I wouldn't have ever guessed that we would wind up here after that disastrous first date, for which I will be eternally sorry, my dear. But I am very grateful that you stuck with me through all the hardships, because if you hadn't, we would never know how much happiness we have in each other, and nothing in my life has ever made me as happy as you have." He smiled at her and kissed her back.

The months that followed found their families bonded together through their marriage and through a very mutually beneficial business collaboration. In time, Reed and Jillian learned to operate Carter's business and they even found ways to streamline it and make it grow much stronger and faster than it had before.

After they had been married two years, they welcomed a son and a year after that, Jillian gave birth to a daughter. They built their family on love, trust, and faith in each other, and that foundation made a strong and lasting, loving family **that thrived until the end of their days.**

THE END

Hey beautiful!

I really hope you enjoyed my novel and I would really love if you could give me a rating on the store!

Thanks in advance and check the next page for details of my other releases. :)

CJ x x

ALSO BY CJ HOWARD

THE BILLIONAIRE'S LOVE CHILD

On the surface, Billionaire Kevin has it all. He is rich beyond his wildest dreams and has the perfect trophy wife to go with it.

However, there is one thing he wants more then anything else in the world... A Child.

Only problem is, his wife refuses to give him any children and does not have any plans to do so ever. A divorce would be too messy for a man of his wealth so Kevin has no choice but to take drastic action.

He hires a surrogate with a **TWIST**.

He will father a baby with her but in this arrangement she will get to keep it. In return, mother and child will be supported financially for the rest of their lives. They will never need or want for anything, just as long as Kevin can fulfill his dream of being a dad.

For the beautiful and curvy Marina this is the ideal arrangement for her. She has always dreamed of being a mother but has never met a man worthy.

Kevin and Marina are about to embark on a very unique arrangement. One that promises to blur the line between love and convenience. Can such an arrangement exist without feelings getting involved? And can Kevin really stand by and watch his love child grow up without being involved directly?

AVAILABLE NOW!

Manufactured by Amazon.ca
Acheson, AB